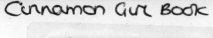
Cinnamon Girl

This Way
To Paradise

Cathy Hopkins is the author of the incredibly successful *Mates, Dates* and *Truth, Dare* books, and has just started a fabulous new series called *Cinnamon Girl*. She lives in North London with her husband and three cats, Molly, Emmylou and Otis.

Cathy spends most of her time locked in a shed at the bottom of the garden pretending to write books but is actually in there listening to music, hippie dancing and talking to her friends on e-mail.

Occasionally she is joined by Molly, the cat who thinks she is a copy-editor and likes to walk all over the keyboard rewriting and deleting any words she doesn't like.

Emmylou and Otis are new to the household. So far they are as insane as the older one. Their favourite game is to run from one side of the house to the other as fast as possible, then see if they can fly if they leap high enough off the furniture. This usually happens at three o'clock in the morning and they land on anyone who happens to be asleep at the time.

Apart from that, Cathy has joined the gym and spends more time than is good for her making up excuses as to why she hasn't got time to go.

Cathy Hopkins

Cinnamon Girl

This Way
To Paradise

PICCADILLY PRESS * LONDON

I'd like to dedicate this to my mum, Clare Hopkins with love.
Thanks also to Steve Lovering for patiently listening to me talk
through every aspect of this book morning, noon and night.
Thanks to Brenda Gardner as always and especially to
Anne Clark for her wonderfully constructive feedback,
plus all the fab team at Piccadilly.

First published in Great Britain in 2007
by Piccadilly Press Ltd,
5 Castle Road, London NW1 8PR
www.piccadillypress.co.uk

Text copyright © Cathy Hopkins, 2007

A catalogue record for this book is available from the British Library

ISBN-13: 978 1 85340 900 4 (trade paperback)

1 3 5 7 9 10 8 6 4 2

Printed and bound in Great Britain by Bookmarque Ltd
Typeset by Carolyn Griffiths, Cambridge
Cover design by Simon Davis

Set in 11.5 Bembo and Tempus

Chapter 1

Sham-pooh!

'We're here,' I said into the phone as I flopped on to my bed. I'd positioned it next to the window so that I could lie and look up at the clear July sky or sit and look down at what was happening on the street below.

'What's it like?' asked Erin at the other end of the phone.

'Heaven. Magic. Totally fab,' I said as I took in the view of the trees and roof tops of the houses opposite.

'Boys?'

'Give me a break! I've only been here half a day.'

'That's long enough. You're slacking, India Jane. What have you been doing?'

'Getting here, Miss Bossy Boots. Unpacking my stuff. What else?'

1

'Pff,' said Erin. 'Get your priorities straight, girl. I'd be straight out and off down Portobello Road, checking out the local talent.'

'I will. I promise. As soon as I can and I'm sorry I haven't had a chance to do a proper recce yet but, from what I've seen so far, I have to say that it's looking good. Aunt Sarah's house is only a couple of streets away from Notting Hill tube and when we drove past there, I did see a few contenders.'

'I am soooo jealous,' said Erin. 'Only you would get to live in deepest trendyville. I so wish I was there with you in London instead of stuck over here in leprechaun land.'

'Me too. You could always run away. I'm sure Mum and Dad wouldn't mind. You know what they're like. Mr and Mrs Liberal. They've already adopted an orang-utan in Malaysia, a donkey in Devon and a goat in Africa. A run-away teenage girl would give them a complete set.'

'Don't be cynical,' said Erin. 'Your parents are top. I like that they give to good causes. Shows they care about stuff.'

'Well, I suppose that we can be grateful that at least the goat, donkey and orang-utan aren't here with us. Seems like everyone else is. I escaped straight up to my room for a bit of peace. It's mad downstairs. Dad's bossing everyone around in his usual manner. They're all here "helping" with the move, but actually getting in the way.'

'Who? Who's there?'

'Ethan, his wife Jessica, Lewis, Dylan, Aunt Sarah, of course, and I saw my cousin Kate for a second, but she was off somewhere in a hurry as always. Ethan and Jess brought the twins too. Ethan's been training them to say, "We are the evil twins. The daughters of Satan." It's so funny because they're so cute and angelic-looking with great blue eyes and curly hair. They're not much help with the unpacking though. Ethan —'

'Ah, Ethan, swoon, swoon. Is he still gorgeous and a half?'

'He is – and way too old for you.'

'No, he's not. I'm fifteen.'

'Yeah and he's twenty-eight and married and, before you say anything, Lewis is also too old for you.'

Ethan is my step-brother from Dad's first marriage. He had come over to welcome us to the big city, as had Lewis. Dylan (who's twelve) and Lewis are my real brothers, but Lewis won't be living with us as he is a student and has digs up in Crouch End in North London.

'Nah, Lewis is a baby,' said Erin. 'He's only nineteen, isn't he?'

I laughed. Just before my family left Ireland, Erin decided that she was into older men. Like, at least twenty. I can see her point – as boys of our age do act immature most of the time, but I think that older boys can be difficult as well. Like in the trying it on department (and I don't mean trying on clothes).

'OK. Now, tell me everything,' said Erin. 'I want to be able to see it all in my head so, when we talk or e-mail, I can imagine exactly what it looks like. Start with the front door, no, start before that. At the front gate. On the street. Give me details.'

'OK,' I said. 'Details. Holland Park. *Très chic* —'

'Who picked you up at the airport?' Erin interrupted.

'Aunt Sarah.'

'In what?'

'She's got a new black BMW. She's loaded, don't forget.'

'Then what?'

'We came straight here. Took just over an hour. The traffic is something else.'

'Weather in Londinium?'

'Lovely. A beautiful summer's day. Not a cloud in the sky. What's it like over there in Kilkerry?'

'Duh. Raining, of course.'

'Of course.' I knew all about the rain in Ireland. For the duration of our two years over there, my parents had rented a castle. They liked living in interesting locations. All my life we've stayed in unusual places, and the castle was beautiful, no doubt about that, stunning in fact and a nice enough place to live when the weather was good, which was hardly ever. It really does rain a lot in that part of Ireland and the castle leaked. We were forever running around with bowls, pots and pans to catch the relentless drips. I even woke up one morning to find a hole in the ceiling in my room and a mini waterfall gushing through. It's an aspect of living there that I'm not going to miss, which is why it's so heavenly to be at Aunt Sarah's. As well as being loaded, she is organised, stylish and together in a way that my mum can only watch in wonder. No leaks in her gaff. Oh no.

All surfaces, walls and ceilings are sealed, damp-proofed and painted in tasteful shades of designer paint. Not that Mum isn't stylish, she is in her own boho-waif way. It's the organised and together bit she's not good at. Nor is Dad, for that matter. They're like Peter Pan and Wendy. I sometimes wonder how the two have them have managed so far. Actually, I know exactly how. Grandpa's inheritance, that's how. The inheritance which has now run out, hence our moving in with Mum's sister and her daughter, Kate.

'The house is a dream, Erin, I'll take some pics and e-mail them to you. It'll be better if you can see for yourself.'

'Just tell me a bit to give me a rough idea.'

'OK. It's tall, cream and *très chic*. Five storey, like most of the houses in the street are. Six bedrooms, three reception rooms and a private studio at the bottom of the back garden that Aunt Sarah uses as her office. Dylan and I are on the top floor and we have our own bathroom with the most amazing power shower that has a nozzle head thingee as big as a football. Kate's room is on the second floor and next to it a spare guest room and another bathroom. Aunt Sarah and Mum and Dad's rooms are on the first. All the rooms are huge and light with high ceilings, big windows and wooden floors. She's done it out in neutral tones and added colour with all her knick knacks, rugs and bits and pieces from places she's visited around the world – mainly Thailand and India, I think.'

'Sounds wonderful.'

'It is. The only rooms that are a bit dark are the basement, and the kitchen – which is at the back of the house. It's tall and narrow and has one of those ancient pulley drying-racks hanging from the ceiling. People used them in olden days to hang their washing on before they had machines and dryers.'

'Is that how your aunt dries her washing then?'

'No way. She uses it to hang her pans and utensils on. It's brilliant – you can haul them right up out of the way. You'll see it when you come over later in the summer. '

'I can't wait. What's your room like?'

'Pretty. Simple seaside colours. Sky blue and pale sand. Aunt Sarah said I can put what I like on the wall to make me feel at home. I carried the pic of us two over in my hand luggage. It's the first thing I put out in here.'

'And so it should be. The one we had taken in Dublin?'

'Yeah.'

The photo of Erin and me was taken at a train station in Dublin when we were on a school trip a few weeks before I left. I'd had the photo blown up so that it would fill a silver frame that Grannie Ruspoli gave me one Christmas. Erin is pushing her nose up with one of her fingers and has gone cross-eyed and I'm sitting behind her doing my zombie face. Not our most attractive picture together, but I liked it because it reminded me of what a laugh we always have. In reality, Erin is tomboyish-looking with an elfin face and short honey-blond hair. She lives in jeans and Converse All Stars (after I turned her on to them). All the boys back in Ireland fancy her. Not that she fancies them back, apart from Scott Malone – the top cutie at our school, who everyone fancies. She is very picky and says she'd rather wait for the right one than compromise. That only makes boys chase her more, as boys like a challenge (according to my brothers).

'You going to be OK, then?' asked Erin.

'Yeah. Hope so. I still feel nervous about starting a new school in September. I'm going to *so* hate being the new girl again.'

'You'll be fine. You're a babe, plus you're a Gemini. They're one of the best star signs for making new friends. People will be falling over themselves to get in with you.'

'Yeah, right. Just like everyone was when I started at your school. Not. We didn't become mates for almost a year.'

'Ah well, I'm a Taurian. We like to take time to make up our minds about people but, when we do, we're very loyal.'

'I know. Now, I can't get rid of you. God knows I've tried! I mean, look, I've moved country and yet you're still calling me.'

Erin laughed at the other end. 'I'm going to go now. I'm not going to take those kind of insults from a low life like you. Actually I do have to go, Dad's calling. He wants me to wash the car, like, sometimes I wonder what his last slave died of. Anyway, e-mail or text and send pics of boys and the house. OK?'

'Will do.'

'Actually, wait a mo, India J. Before you go, I'm going to give you some homework.'

'Homework?'

'Yes. You have to go out today some time and take a pic of the cutest boy you see then e-mail it to me, OK?'

'Yes sir, sergeant major, SIR!'

'Dismissed,' said Erin and hung up.

After I'd put the phone down, I was about to start unpacking when I heard Mum calling me from downstairs.

I went down to see what she wanted and found her in the hall. She looked flustered. 'You haven't seen my purse, have you?"

I shook my head.

'We need milk, sweetheart,' she continued as she searched the hallway for her bag. 'With all these extra people here, it's all gone. Would you be a love and pop out and get us some?'

'But I don't know where to get it,' I protested.

'Then find out,' said Dad, bursting into the hall from the kitchen and overhearing the last part of our conversation. Dad never enters a room. He always *bursts* in like a tornado, creating commotion and noise in his wake – partly because he's a big man, a presence, and partly because of his larger-than-life personality. 'You'll have to find your way soon enough.'

'But . . .' I was about to object then realised that there was no point. It was typical of Dad to make me go out into a strange place on my own. It wouldn't occur to him that I might feel wary of the area until I knew my way around more. It's like how he taught us to swim. He threw us in at the deep end. It was only when Dylan looked like he was drowning that Dad realised that sometimes it's better to be cautious. Dad's totally insensitive to new things and change. He loves it. Thrives on it. Sees it all as one big adventure and, because he does, he thinks the rest of us do. Hence the five different places I'd lived in by my fifteenth birthday.

Aunt Sarah came into the hall after Dad. Nobody would ever know that she and Mum were sisters to look at them. Mum takes after my late grandmother, who was a typical English rose, and Aunt Sarah takes after Grandpa, who was short and stocky. Mum is tall and willowy with delicate features, whereas Aunt Sarah is smaller and curvier. With her dark hair, she looks more like she could be related to Dad's family, who are Italian. Both Mum and Aunt Sarah are into the 'designer hippie' look, though, and favour clothes and accessories from the Far East, which is pretty cool for me as I like a lot of that stuff too.

'Where can India Jane get milk?' asked Dad.

'Out to the street, turn left, down to the lights, over the road and there's a mini mart next to Starbucks,' said Aunt Sarah.

'Excellent,' said Dad. 'India will find it, won't you?'

'But I can't find my purse,' said Mum.

Aunt Sarah sighed, found her bag and gave me a ten pound note.

'And can you pop into a chemist's and get me some shampoo?' asked Dad. 'Any old kind will do. Thanks, angel.'

I quickly ran back upstairs to put some shoes on, then spent a few minutes getting ready. After all, it was my first venture out into deepest trendyville, as Erin had called it. I opened one of the suitcases that hadn't been unpacked yet and threw a few things out on to the floor. I pulled off the T-shirt I was wearing, put my cinnamon-coloured wrap-around dress on over my jeans and slung a brown leather belt and a silver Indian belt around my hips. I checked my appearance in the long mirror to the left of the door. A tall slim girl with brown eyes, long chestnut hair and copper highlights looked back at me. Was the dress over jeans a look that was 'over' here in London? I wondered. It was a fashion that had been in and out a few times in the last few years. Erin and I liked the look and we also always wore two belts regardless of whether the mags said it was in or out. I liked to pick items of fashion from different eras and sling them together to make my own look. I wound my hair up and fixed it in place with the red and black lacquered chopstick I always used. A slick of Brick lippie and I was ready.

'India Jane, people are waiting for their tea,' Dad called up the stairs.

That's another thing Dad is. Impatient. Always wants everything yesterday.

I grabbed my digi-cam in case I saw any boys to e-mail to Erin and hurtled back down the stairs and out of the door.

I followed Aunt Sarah's instructions and soon saw the shops that I was to go to. It felt good to be out on such a lovely day and feel the sun on my skin. My spirits rose further as a couple of cute boys on bikes rode past and waved at me. I was so looking forward to living in London. I'd been before when we'd come over to stay with Aunt Sarah, but we'd never stayed longer than a week and the last time we'd visited had been years ago. This time we'd be living here and I couldn't wait to explore and see what was out there.

As I passed by Starbucks, I immediately noticed a boy sitting in the window talking on his mobile phone. I quickly whipped out my shades and put them on so that I could look again without him knowing that I was specifically ogling him. He was *exactly* my type, which was amazing because I had never seen my type in the flesh before – only in movies or magazines. He was wearing black jeans and a T-shirt and was talking animatedly to the person on the other end of his phone. If he was typical of London boys, things were looking good. As I focused on him behind my glasses, I confirmed to myself that he was *über* good-looking: medium height, slim with shoulder-length brown hair with a slight curl, and a great bone structure. I always notice things like that because I want to be an artist, and drawing people's faces is what I like doing best. As he finished his call and looked out of the window, his expression became moody as if he was thinking hard about something or someone. *Erin would just die if I sent a pic of him,* I thought. She had a pin-up on her wall of an actor from the 1950s called James Dean. He was in a film called *Rebel Without a Cause* and this boy had the same expression on his face as James Dean had in the poster – sort of moody, broody and dangerous. I positioned myself at the bus stop outside the café and aimed my camera as if I was taking a general shot of the front of the building. At the very last minute, I aimed it at the boy and clicked.

I checked to see the shot and, bingo, it was perfect. Erin was going to be so jealous and this was only my first day. I clicked the camera shut and glanced back into the window. The boy was staring straight at me. As our eyes met, I felt a butterfly flutter in my stomach. I quickly turned away, walked towards the general store and reassured myself that he couldn't have known that I was looking at him as I had my shades on. They're big and black. No one could see through them. Erin and I had tested them before I bought them in Ireland.

When I reached the mini mart, I took off my glasses, bought the milk and a chocolate bar then went into the chemist's for Dad's shampoo.

There was the usual array for different types of hair – dry, greasy, frizzy, coloured, damaged. Shampoos with fruits, herbs, aloe vera, all sorts of magic ingredients. In the end, I grabbed one that was an attractive blue colour and headed for the till. An old lady was in front of me and, as I was waiting, I looked around the shop for future reference.

The shop door opened and the boy from Starbucks came in. I quickly looked away but not before I noticed that he was taller than he'd looked in the café. Out of the corner of my eye, I could see that he went over to a shelf to the right and began looking at toothbrushes. He picked one out and headed to the counter and stood behind me. I turned away as I didn't want to be caught staring. Instead, I studied the display on the counter in front of me.

The Indian man who was serving finished with the old lady then nodded at the boy behind me.

'Hi, Joe,' he said.

'Hey, Mr Patel,' said the boy and he held up his toothbrush, 'for my trip.'

'Lucky you,' said Mr Patel.

'Yep. Gonna be away for most of the summer.'

Mr Patel nodded. 'I know. Your mother was in earlier buying up supplies too. When are you going?'

'Next week,' said Joe, 'although Mum's going earlier – but, hey, this girl was in front of me, weren't you?'

It was only then that I realised that the items I had been pretending to be so engrossed in were pregnancy tests and it looked as if Joe had noticed. I felt the back of my neck grow warm. 'Er . . . yes, no . . . no, you go ahead,' I blustered. 'No hurry.'

Joe glanced down at the pregnancy tests. 'Sure?' he asked.

'*Quate* sure,' I said in a voice that sounded like the Queen.

'No, please, you go,' said Joe. 'You were here first.'

I held out the shampoo to Mr Patel, who took it then

said, 'We have combs that go with this shampoo.'

'That's OK, I have a hairbrush,' I said. I felt my face go pink as I sensed that Joe was listening.

'Ah, but brushes are no good at all for head lice,' said Mr Patel. 'You need a fine comb to catch the eggs they've laid. Is the shampoo for you?'

Behind me, Joe took a couple of steps back.

I felt myself turn from pink to red. 'Head *lice*!? No way. I . . .'

I glanced down at the bottle. *For head lice*, it said clearly on the label. I hadn't noticed the writing when I'd grabbed it from the shelf. I instinctively put my hand up to my head and Joe stepped back even further. 'I . . . *No*. Really. It's not for me. I mean . . . I haven't got head lice.'

'No need to be ashamed, my dear,' said the chemist. 'It is very common.'

'No, really . . .' I began to protest.

'So who's the shampoo for?' asked Mr Patel.

'My dad. That is . . . nooooo, he —'

'Ah, your dad,' interrupted Mr Patel, 'even so, it's best if all the family use the shampoo. Head lice spread so fast.'

'But I . . . I mean, neither he nor we have got head lice. *None* of my family have got them.'

I dared to take a quick glance at Joe who had moved behind a make-up display and had an 'oh yeah, pull the other one' look on his face.

'We *really* haven't,' I said to him. 'No need to hide!'

Joe held up his hands and shrugged. 'Woah, just standing in the queue here.'

I quickly went back over to the hair product display, put the head lice shampoo back on the shelf, got a Fruits of the Forest for normal hair and took it back to the counter. 'I'll have this instead,' I said. 'It *is* for my dad. NOT for me. And he has totally normal hair. As in NORMAL, no head lice.'

I heard Joe chuckle behind me.

I paid for my shampoo and headed for the door. As I opened it to leave, I could hear both Joe *and* Mr Patel laughing.

As I stomped back up the road, I thought, *Talk about making a good first impression. Possibly pregnant with head lice. I really, really hope that I never bump into that boy ever again. Thank God he's going on a trip somewhere. The further the better.*

Chapter 2

Kissing Cousin

'Wow,' said Kate as she flipped through the paintings in the folder leaning up against the wall opposite my bed. 'Who did these?'

'Oh. Me.'

'They're fantastic, India Jane. I never knew you were so good at art.'

'Oh . . . thanks. They're not really that good – I prefer doing people.'

There were five paintings. All landscapes. The first was a hotel by Lake Picola, Udaipur in India. The second a palazzo in Venice. Third was a beach house in St Lucia in the Caribbean, fourth a villa in Essaouira in Morocco and last, the castle in Ireland. They were the five places I'd lived since I was born. For my art project last year, we were asked to paint where we lived. Most people painted one place, two at the most, mainly grey scenes depicting a typical Irish house. Mine looked like a display in a travel agent's. Erin made copies for her bedroom wall to join her poster of James Dean. 'To aspire to,' she said. One of her goals in life is to travel. All I've ever wanted is to stay in one place and have a proper home.

'Hey, don't be modest,' said Kate. 'They're great. You've got to put them up on the wall. I wish I was good at art. I wish I was good at anything. I am, like, so totally dreading my exam results. Mum's going to blow a fuse if I haven't done well.'

'She'll be in Greece when they come through, won't she?'

Kate mock strangled herself. 'Yeah, but the wrath of the Killer Mom can be felt anywhere on the planet. I am so happy that you guys have moved in with us. If you hadn't, she'd have made me go with her like last summer and the one before, but thanks to your mum and dad, responsible adults and all that —'

'Hardly,' I interrupted.

'Well, don't tell Mum that. She's cool with them being around to keep an eye on me so to speak, which means I can stay and hang out with my mates.'

'I'd have thought you'd have liked the idea of a summer in Greece.'

Kate shook her head. 'Nah. Not my scene. Been there, done that. I like London.'

'Me too.'

This morning was the first time that I'd seen my cousin properly since we'd arrived in London three days ago, as she'd always been out late or in a hurry to get somewhere. At last, she'd come up to my room for 'a nose' as she said. She'd stayed over with a mate of hers in Chelsea last night and was well in the doghouse with her mum, who was leaving for Greece later in the day. Her absence meant that they didn't have much time together before Aunt Sarah left (which I reckoned was exactly what Kate intended). I liked Kate a lot. At seventeen, she's a couple of years older than me and is way cool. She has the look of a ballet dancer, tall and lean with not an ounce of fat on her although she never exercises and claims that she is totally unfit. She paints her nails in electric-blue glitter polish, dresses only in black, and she wears the most fab pair of Prada sunglasses when she's out, and sometimes even when she's in, much to her mother's annoyance. They seem to have been cross with each other since as far back as I can remember. Kate reckons that the reason is because she looks like her dad and is a constant reminder of him – something that her mum doesn't want, since they split up when Kate was eight. Aunt Sarah was forever complaining that Kate should wear 'some colour'. She bought her the most gorgeous stuff from Harvey Nichols in Knightsbridge as an end of her exams present, but Kate just turned her nose up and pronounced the clothes as 'too girlie'. I wouldn't have. I think Aunt Sarah has fab taste, but Kate wouldn't back down.

She sat at my dressing table, picked up one of my combs and pulled her long dark hair back up into it. As she did so, I noticed that she had a lovebite on the side of her neck.

'Oh Christ,' she sighed as she looked at it in the mirror. 'I'll kill that Jamie Morris. Is it really noticeable?'

I nodded.

'Got any cover-up?'

'For spots.'

'That'll do.'

'In the left-hand drawer.'

Kate pulled open the drawer and found my concealer. 'Thanks,' she said as she applied it and then let her hair out of the clip so that it fell loosely around her shoulders again. 'You settled in OK?'

'Yeah.'

I'd spent the last few days unpacking and already my room looked like home. I'd put my aquamarine velvet throw over the bed with a couple of the sequined indigo cushions that Mum had got years ago in a market in Goa. Over the rail, at the top of the window, I'd hung a turquoise sari (another Goa purchase) and, overall, the colours went beautifully with the blue Aunt Sarah had chosen for the walls. Lastly, I'd put the Venetian glass mirror that Mum and Dad got me one birthday on the dressing table then draped all my beads and necklaces over one corner.

Kate got up, pulled a packet of Marlboro Lights out of her jean pockets, knelt on my bed to open the window and then lit up a cigarette.

'Want one?' she asked.

I shook my head. I'd tried smoking with Erin at a Christmas party last year. Both of us thought they tasted foul, and mine made my head swim and I felt like I was going to throw up. Later that same evening, Erin got off with Scott Malone. Just as they started snogging, he backed off and said he didn't like kissing girls who smoked as it made their mouths sour. Erin was mortified and tried to tell him that she wasn't really a smoker but he said 'yeah, right' and went and got off with Tracey Ingram. Neither of us tried fags again after that.

As she smoked her cigarette, Kate looked at the bedside cabinet where I'd put my two framed photos. I'd carried them over in my hand luggage on the plane so that the glass didn't break. One showed the family sitting round the table on the terrace at Grannie Ruspoli's, when we were together last year in Italy for Dad's fiftieth birthday. Ethan and Lewis take after Dad: handsome with a mane of wild dark hair, olive skin and amber eyes. Dylan is more like Mum and has her pale English complexion and fine features. I'm a mixture of Mum and Dad. I have olive skin like him, his amber eyes and chestnut red hair, which is a couple of shades darker than Mum's. When I was little, I was a total Daddy's girl. I adored him and followed him everywhere and, if he ever went out, I'd wait by the door like a faithful puppy until he returned. Of course I grew out of that ages ago, and these days we clash probably more than anyone else in the family. I'm not his obedient little pet any more. It annoys me the way he always wants, and gets, his own way about everything and Mum just goes along with it like she has no opinion of her own. My brothers let him have his own way too. He's their hero. Dad calls me Cinnamon Girl because of my colouring. He got the expression from a song back in the sixties by Neil Young. For my birthday every year, Mum makes a special perfume from cinnamon oil and a few other ingredients that I don't know (she won't tell as she says it is her secret formula). It smells totally amazing – warm and spicy – and, when I wear it, people always ask where they can get some.

'Your mum and dad look beautiful in the photo,' said Kate, 'like a prince and princess from a fairy story. Mind you, your whole family are lookers. You all have the same fabulous heart-shaped faces. Seems your mum and dad have passed on the best of their looks combined.'

What a lovely thing to say, I thought as I nodded. Mum and Dad were always telling me that I was *bella*, beautiful, but then, being my parents, they're biased. Not many other people have said anything about my looks, so it was really nice to hear it from someone like Kate.

'Your dad is a prince, isn't he?

'Almost. He's a count. Dad doesn't use his title though. He says that, when people hear that he is a count, they expect him to be rich, which he isn't so, in order to avoid explanations, he simply doesn't tell anyone.'

'So what happened to the family dosh?'

'One of his ancestors gambled it away so that all the family have left is the title.'

'Shame,' said Kate, then she picked up the second photo of Erin and me on the school trip. 'Whose the mad girl in the pic?'

I laughed. 'Erin,' I said, as we heard the sound of the doorbell. 'She's my mate back in Ireland.'

'She looks like a laugh,' said Kate.

'She was. Is. The photo doesn't do her justice. We were messing around. She's really very pretty.'

The doorbell rang again.

'Someone downstairs will get it,' said Kate, who continued smoking and poking around my room.

A few minutes later, the bell rang again.

'Honestly,' said Kate. 'No one ever answers the door in this place. Or the phone.'

I went over to the window and peered out to see if I could see anyone. It was raining outside and whoever it was downstairs was hidden under an umbrella. 'I guess one of us could go,' I said.

'Why should we when we're up here at the top of the house and they're down there on the ground?'

'Actually, I think Mum and Dylan have gone out shopping,' I said. 'And Dad was going to see an old friend of his about some work and er . . . your mum's taking a shower.'

Kate shrugged. 'Well, I'm not expecting anyone. Are you?'

'No. I don't know anyone here.'

22

The doorbell rang again. A long insistent ring.

'Look. I'll get it,' I said, when it became clear that Kate wasn't going to go. 'I don't mind.'

Kate pulled my new copy of *Teen Vogue* magazine from the shelf above my desk, then went and lay back on my bed. 'Suit yourself,' she said. 'It's probably someone selling something.'

I flew down the stairs two at a time, raced to the door and opened it just in time to see the back of someone heading for the gate.

'Hi. Sorry,' I called. 'Can I help you?'

The person turned and lowered the umbrella.

It was the boy from the mini mart. Joe.

Chapter 3

Sniffer Dog

Footsteps stomped angrily down the stairs. A second later, the kitchen door burst open.

'HAVE YOU BEEN SMOKING UP IN YOUR ROOM?'

I was about to bite into a slice of wholemeal toast spread with raspberry jam and crunchy peanut butter (my favourite combo) but stopped pre-chomp. 'Not me, honest —' I began, then thought, *Why am I explaining myself to my TWELVE-year-old brother?* 'Not that it's any of your business.'

'It *is* my business,' he said. 'I share that floor with you, and people have been known to die of passive smoking.'

His expression was so earnest that it made me want to laugh. 'So bite me,' I said with a grin. 'Like, what were you in your last life? A sniffer dog?'

'It's *not* a joke, India Jane,' he said. 'Statistics show —'

'Statistics *show*,' I mimicked, causing Dylan to look even crosser. 'Get yourself an oxygen mask. I can do what I like, and have who I like in my room, and they can do what they like when they're up there.'

Dylan clenched his teeth, gave me a filthy look, then went out slamming the door behind him.

'Stress can kill you too,' I called after him.

Inwardly, I cursed that I hadn't thought to light a joss stick before he and Mum got back. As soon as Joe had gone, I'd raced back upstairs to ask Kate for the low down on who he was, but all that was left of her was the lingering smell of cigarette smoke. When I came looking for her downstairs, I got distracted by my rumbly tummy and got involved making toast before fumigating my room. Of course, Dylan the Nose had sniffed out the whiff of cigarettes as soon as he'd gone up there.

A moment later, Mum appeared, put some groceries in the fridge, then disappeared again. She'd probably smelled the smoke too when she went upstairs as it had permeated the whole house, but she didn't say anything. She wouldn't. Mum and Dad believe in letting us experiment and find our own way. Unlike Dylan. He's a bit of an old lady when it comes to health, like he's the conscience for our whole family. He's forever lecturing us about the dangers of preservatives, additives, too much sugar or salt. He's not normal, that's for sure, or maybe it's because he's a Scorpio and they are supposed to be intense. I reckon it's also because he's small for his age. Something he hates. Erin said that he overcompensates for his size like small dogs do by making a lot of noise. He doesn't need to worry. Both Mum and Dad are tall, so he'll probably grow eventually but sadly not soon enough for him. Personally, I don't know why he gets so het up about everything. Mum and Dad are health conscious, always have been, and they have always bought organic food, even grown it where they could. But they're chilled about it. Not Dylan though. He looks at the back of packages, checks all the ingredients. He's obsessive. I sometimes wonder how he manages to make friends. He does though, especially with girls – as he is cute, even though a tad short at the moment. Back in Ireland, there was always a bunch of coy girls on the phone for him or waiting for him at the school gate.

Upstairs, I could hear Kate and Aunt Sarah rowing about something. She'd probably smelled the smoke too and unlike Dylan wasn't blaming me. *Oh happy families,* I thought as I got my phone out and texted Erin.

Hey. M in luv. India J XX

A text came straight back.

Who? Wen? Where? How?

I was about to text again when Kate burst into the kitchen.

'Christ,' she sighed and looked at her watch. 'Only two hours before Monster Mother goes – then peace.' She eyed the second piece of toast, jam and peanut butter that was lying on my plate ready to be eaten, picked it up and took a bite.

'Um . . . Kate,' I said. 'That boy who came to the door before . . .'

'What boy?'

'Joe. I think his name's Joe. He dropped an envelope off for your mum.'

Kate shrugged. 'Oh Joe Donahue. Yeah. What about him?'

'Who is he?'

Kate stopped chewing, sat down opposite and scrutinised me with narrow eyes. 'Do you fancy him?'

I felt myself redden. 'Er . . . maybe. I don't really know him.'

'Oh God,' said Kate, then she shook her head. 'Don't. Not Joe. He's in the same year as me at school. Stay away from him.'

'Why? He looked nice.'

'Don't all the bad boys?'

'Bad boy? Why?'

Kate tapped the side of her nose. 'Just trust me on this,' she said. 'And I know it may sound rich coming from me, seeing as I have had my fair share of bad-boy boyfriends but, believe me, Joe Donahue is in a league of his own and no way do I want to see you hurt.'

I was about to ask her more, but Mum came back in with more groceries and I didn't want her getting into it and then later it becoming a topic of conversation for the whole family. *I'll corner Kate later,* I thought, *and find out more.* I was intrigued. He hadn't seemed like bad news at the door earlier. At first I couldn't believe my eyes when I saw that he was standing there on Aunt Sarah's front steps, looking even more handsome than before with his hair damp and slightly curled from the rain. I think my jaw must have fallen open and he looked amused when he saw that it was me.

He'd glanced up at the house. 'Can you give this to Sarah . . . that is Mrs Rosen.'

'Sure. She's my aunt,' I said.

'Ah,' he said and a twinkle appeared in his eyes. 'And part of the family that *hasn't* got head lice?'

'The very same,' I said in a stupidly pompous manner for which I immediately cursed myself. 'I . . . I picked up the wrong bottle by mistake.'

'Easily done,' he said and gave me a killer-watt smile.

I scanned my brain for something witty and brilliant to say back but all that came out was, 'Yumph.'

He nodded as if I'd said something sensible. 'Er yeah. OK. Later then,' he said and for a few seconds our eyes met and my stomach did the fluttery butterfly thing again. There was a connection and I was sure he'd felt it too.

He turned back into the rain, put his umbrella up, walked down the path, out the gate and disappeared. I wanted to yell after him – later *when* exactly? Where are you going on your trip? How long for? Who with? When are you back? Do you have a girlfriend? Do you want one?

But of course, I didn't.

'Yeah, later,' I said into the rain.

As soon as Aunt Sarah's taxi had gone, Kate started making her own plans to leave, but I cornered her in the hall before she escaped.

'See yus,' she said as she donned her Prada glasses, shoved a twenty pound note into the back pocket of her jeans and headed for the front door.

'I . . . but . . . just before you go, I wanted to ask you more about Joe,' I blustered.

She rolled her eyes up to the ceiling. 'I told you, he's bad news. There's a trail of broken hearts after that boy and, seeing as I am your older responsible cousin, I'm going to make sure that yours isn't one of them.'

Personally I didn't think that 'Kate' and 'responsible' were two words that went together but I wasn't going to spoil her moment of feeling protective towards me.

'Well, he's going on a trip,' I said. 'So not much chance of anything happening.'

Kate nodded. 'He's going to Greece.'

'What? With Aunt Sarah?'

'Yes. No. At least, he's not travelling with her. He's going out soon though, I think. Not sure when.'

'How come?'

'His mum's one of my mum's oldest friends. Her name's Charlotte, but we call her Lottie. They go back years. She helped Mum set up the centre and she runs workshops over there.'

'Really. What kind?'

'Get bendy, stick your leg behind your left ear and get enlightened type tosh, you know – yoga. And she does bore-yourself-into-oblivion nutrition too, I think. Lentils and brown rice. To be avoided at all costs.'

I burst out laughing. 'Not quite how they describe it in the brochure,' I said.

The centre in Greece, called Cloud Nine, was Aunt Sarah's latest business venture. Unlike my mum, who used her inheritance to travel the world, Aunt Sarah had invested hers. First she had a stall on Portobello Road selling jewellery that she'd bought in India and Thailand. With the proceeds from that, she bought a small shop and then another and then another, until she had four shops selling jewellery and artefacts from all over the world. Next, she invested in property and bought the house in Holland Park, plus a couple of flats in North London that she rented out. A few years ago, she sold the flats, bought land in Greece and set up a centre for holistic holidays. It offers all sorts of self-help and creative workshops, and people go there to do writing, art, meditation, dance, yoga – a variety of classes from the weird to the wonderful.

Kate laughed too. 'Yeah. Mum ought to ask me to do the

blurb for her. I'd tell the truth about what goes on there. Not my idea of fun, I can tell you that much.'

'So why's Joe going then? What's he going to do there?'

Kate shrugged. 'Dunno. Not to do the classes. I think I heard Mum say something about getting him a job out there for the summer. In the town not the centre. But he's probably going mainly so that Lottie can keep an eye on him. Which means the big bad wolf is out of the way for the summer and you are safe.'

Yeah, maybe, I thought as Kate made her exit, *but he'd be back in time for school in September.* And the good news was that I'd be going to the same school as him and Kate. Plus my aunt knew his mum. Chances are there would be plenty of opportunity to accidentally bump into him. Later, he'd said. Yeah. I'd make sure that was a definite.

Chapter 4

Change of Plan?

Cinnamongirl: Luv it luv it luv it here. It's fabbie dabbie doobie, Erin. London is so cosmopolitan. Like the whole world is here. All nations. All shapes. All sizes. I've never felt happier and I've got weeks more of it before starting school. I've spent the last few days exploring West London and, the more I've seen, the more I feel like I've died and gone to heaven. High Street Kensington, the posh designer shops in Sloane Street in Knightsbridge, (they even smell expensive – most of them burn the most divine scented candles all day), Portobello Road market which sells everything. You'd love it. Miss U. Wish you were here. India Jane. XXXXXXXXXXXXXXXXXX

Irishbrat4eva: SHUT UP. I hate you. Am too jealous to communicate with you any more. Our friendship is over.

Cinnamongirl: Noooooooooooooooooooooooooooooo. Please be my friend again.

Irishbrat4eva: No. I don't like you any more. I am rinsing you from my life from this moment on. You are far too happy and I am so totally depressed.

Cinnamongirl: Pleeeeeeeeease still be my friend. I do miss you, honest.

Irishbrat4eva: I don't believe you. You've been away for less than a week and already say you have never been happier in your whole life. Clearly I am redundant. You have moved on and not taken me with you. I am going to sulk for the rest of eternity.

OK. Bored with that.

PS. What happened to that boy you were in love with for a nano second? The one whose pic you e-mailed over?

Cinnamongirl: Going to Greece for the summer.

Irishbrat4eva: Ah. Fear not. There will be others. Although he did look cute. Can't wait to come over. Gotta go. Busby's, is calling. Like, see what I mean. You hang out in designer shops in Knightsbridge that smell of expensive perfume. I have to stack shelves in Busby's which smells of old cabbage. Such is my lot in life. BUT NOT FOR LONG!!!!!!!!!!!!!!!!!!!!!!!!!!!!!

33

Erin had got a job for a month in Busby's, which was the local supermarket near where we used to live. She hated it, but it was a way to earn some extra dosh to come over to London in August. It made me think that maybe I should get a part-time job too and earn some money so that I could go and visit her at half-term or Christmas. I knew that Mum and Dad couldn't afford to give me any cash as the only topic of conversation over meals since we had arrived in London was how broke they were and what they were going to do for work. It was going to be a whole new chapter for both of them. Not that either of them had never worked before, just they had never *had* to. Wherever we had been in the world, both of them had always kept busy at something, Dad with his art and music and Mum with her art, jewellery design and homemade bath products.

Finding a job for Mum was no problem. Aunt Sarah had put her to work as soon as she had arrived. Before Aunt Sarah left, she helped Mum to set up a workshop in the basement where she could make jewellery for one of the shops. Aunt Sarah also asked Mum to develop a range of bath soaps, oils and gels, and the house did smell lovely as she experimented with various combinations of herbs, fruits and flowers and their scents wafted up the stairs. Between the posh shops and home, I floated from one lovely smell to another.

Dad wasn't having such an easy time. Although there was loads he could do – as he is good at lots of different things: art, music (he plays piano, cello and guitar) and he speaks a few languages (Italian, Spanish, French and Urdu), he wasn't having much luck finding anyone to employ him. In the first few days in London, he took slides of his paintings around galleries and, although a few expressed interest and one even offered to give him a show, they were all booked up for the next year.

He tried a few of his orchestra friends, but no one had any vacancies except as a stand-in if anyone was sick, but with that there was no promise of regular money.

'Nothing for a Renaissance man like me,' he said and went and took it out on the piano for an hour. That was one of Dad's ways of dealing with problems – make a lot of noise! Although he did play brilliantly sometimes, I longed for the kind of father who had a quieter method of letting off steam.

After we'd been in London a week, Dad blasted out one morning declaring that he was going to the job centre and he was going to take any job there was going. He came back a couple of hours later looking miserable. Really down. I made him a ginger, lemon and honey drink the way he likes and took it to the basement where he had draped himself on an old velvet chaise longue in Mum's workshop.

'No luck?' I asked.

'They offered me a trial job in a DIY store. I'd probably earn no more than your friend Erin, India Jane. Either that or I can work on a building site.'

For the first time I could remember, my bombastic, endlessly enthusiastic dad looked depressed.

'Something will turn up,' said Mum. 'Surely you could teach? Music or languages?'

Dad shook his head. 'I could, but they won't let me. You have to have the right qualifications to work in schools or colleges. And you have to have a CV. A record of employment. The system doesn't allow for people like me. My CV reads like a travel brochure.'

'What about the orchestras?' I asked.

'Nothing happening. No. It will have to be the building site,' he said as he sipped the drink I'd given him and made an attempt at looking brave. 'It'll be fine. All part of life's rich experience and maybe something will turn up in the autumn.'

Thank God for Aunt Sarah's house, I thought as I went back upstairs. *At least we have somewhere to live.*

The following day, Dad went out again and I continued my exploration of the area. I was about to e-mail Erin in the evening about some fabbie dabbie vintage clothing stalls I'd found near Portobello Market, when I heard Dylan yell up the stairs.

'India, INDIAAAAAAAAAAAA JAAAAAAAAAAAAAAAANE!'

I went out on to the landing. 'What?'

'Dad wants us downstairs.'

'What for?'

'Dunno, but he said to come now. Front room.'

Hopefully he's found a job he likes, I thought as I made my way down.

Mum and Dad were seated on one of the huge squashy leather sofas by the fireplace in the front room. Dad grinned cheerfully when I went in.

'Good news?' I asked as I sat next to Dylan on the sofa opposite.

Dad nodded and glanced at Mum. 'Do you want to tell them or shall I?'

'You go ahead,' she said.

Dad gave a brief nod. 'Well, I've got a job.'

'Hurray!' whooped Dylan.

'Fab,' I said. 'Or is it? Is it one you want?'

Dad beamed back at me. 'Oh yes. Couldn't be better. It's with an orchestra. Remember my old friend Robin Beaton?'

Dylan and I nodded. He had been out to see us when we lived in Ireland. He was a pianist with a well known orchestra.

'He's been unwell,' Dad continued, 'and he's going to have to have short spell in hospital and of course will need time for recuperation.'

'Why's he in hospital?' asked Dylan.

'Small op,' Dad replied.

'What exactly?' asked Dylan.

'For prostate cancer,' said Dad.

'Ah,' said Dylan. 'Have they got it in time?'

Mum nodded. 'They think so.'

'Good,' said Dylan, 'because that is one of the cancers that they can do a lot for if it's caught early enough. I saw a programme about it on cable. Tell him he must eat lots of tomatoes.'

Mum and Dad exchanged an amused glance at their son, the health expert.

'Yes,' said Dad. 'It is treatable and luckily they think they've got Robin early enough. The bad news is that he had a whole programme of concerts lined up for over the summer and early autumn. Too late to cancel.'

'He's asked if your father will take his place and fulfil his commitments,' said Mum.

Dylan punched the air. 'Result,' he said.

'Brilliant,' I said.

'I know. Couldn't be better,' said Dad with a huge smile. 'My perfect job, plus I may make connections for the future.'

'So when do you start?' I asked.

'Immediately. First concert is next weekend. It will be good money too.'

I was about to get up when Mum coughed. 'Er India Jane, don't go yet – there's more.'

'Oh right,' I said as I sat back down. 'Hey, we can come and see you perform.'

Dad laughed. 'I doubt that,' he said.

'Why not?' I asked.

'The concerts are all over Europe,' Mum explained.

'Oh,' I said. 'So you'll be away?'

Mum and Dad nodded. 'Yes.'

'And we stay here with Mum?'

Mum glanced at Dad. 'Not exactly. I'm going to go with your father.'

My heart sank. We'd only just got to London and we were going to be off again. 'So when do we leave?' I asked.

'We? Ah, no. Change of plan all round,' said Dad. 'But you'll like it.'

'Your father and I have talked it over,' said Mum, 'and Dylan is going to stay with Ethan for a week.'

'With Ethan?' asked Dylan. 'But is there room for me there with the twins?'

Mum nodded. 'The twins are going to go in with Jessica and you will share with Ethan. Only for a week while I go with your father and help him get settled and then you can come out to join us.'

Dylan beamed at this bit of news as he hero-worshipped his elder step-brother and loved spending time with the twins. 'Cool.'

'Yes,' said Mum. 'I think it will work out perfectly.'

'When will we be back?' asked Dylan.

'At the end of August ready for the new school term,' said Mum. 'Your dad will be back late October.'

Everyone was looking very happy and pleased with themselves at the news. Except me. I felt like someone had knocked me over.

'Er . . . what about me?' I asked.

Dad got up as if the meeting was over. He ran his fingers

through his hair, then looked at his watch. 'You, my darling Cinnamon Girl, you get to go on the holiday of a lifetime.'

Oh God, I thought as the sinking feeling in my chest grew heavier. *How many times have I heard that before he uproots us all for another country. Oh please, please, don't let it be another country.*

'Where exactly?' I asked.

'Your mother spoke to Sarah this afternoon . . .'

Phew, I thought, *so I can stay here with Kate. Wow, that'll be brilliant.* And then I realised that Dad was still talking.

'. . . yes, you'll love it there. Great experience for you.'

'Sorry,' I said. 'Can you rewind a sec. Didn't quite catch that last bit.'

'Greece,' said Dad.

'Greece?' I asked.

'Yes,' said Mum. 'We've decided that you can go and stay with your aunt in Greece. She agreed straight away and as we speak is arranging your flight. Isn't that lovely?'

Dad headed towards the door. 'And so everyone's happy,' he declared. 'I knew it would all work out.'

'Noooooooooooooo,' I said. 'I'm not happy. Please Dad. I want to stay here. I don't want to go to Greece.'

Mum and Dad's faces expressed surprise.

'Why ever not, India Jane?' Dad asked.

'We've only just got here. I *like* it here and I'd like to stay in *one* place for a while,' I blurted.

Dad burst out laughing and tousled my head in a *really*

40

annoying way. 'Nonsense,' he said. 'You'll be fine.' Then he began to sing some Italian opera at the top of his voice. Mum laughed as he left the room and began playing the piano full blast next door. Dylan got up and went to him and, moments later, he could be heard joining in with a tambourine.

'Sometimes I wish this family would just *shut up!*' I muttered.

Mum chuckled as the din from the next room grew louder. 'I know what you mean,' she said.

I knew she didn't.

'It's only to the end of summer and will be a great experience for you,' she said after a few minutes of watching me look gloomily out of the window.

'And so would staying in London,' I said. 'Why can't I stay here with Kate?'

'Out of the question,' said Mum. 'Kate's going to go and stay with her father in Richmond.'

'Why can't *you* stay here then?' I asked.

'Your dad wants me with him. I'll only be gone for the summer. It's a big commitment – he's got a lot to learn in a very short time and will need me with him.'

'I need you with *me*,' I said. 'Why can't you and Dad stay here? He'll get a job soon enough.'

'This is a great chance for him, India,' Mum said. She tried to make me smile by sticking her bottom lip out like I had. I knew I was doing the cliché sulky teenager, but I couldn't help it. And I wasn't going to smile.

'Some teenagers would see a summer in Greece at a place like Sarah's as the opportunity of a lifetime.'

'Then let *them* go,' I said.

I folded my arms across my stomach, crossed my legs and tried to hold back the tears that were threatening to spill over on to my cheeks. Not that Mum noticed. She got up and went to join Dad and Dylan and, a moment later, I could hear the three of them singing along in their happy family sing-song. Mum will never get into an argument. Her way of dealing with rows is to walk away. *No one cares what I want,* I thought. *No one ever does.*

Outside the light began to fade. *Just like my fantasy of the perfect summer in London,* I thought as I got up to go and kick a wall and then IM Erin the latest.

Chapter 5

Never Give Up

Irishbrat4eva: WHAAAAAAAAAAAAAAAAADT? No. This can't happen. I *can't* have been stacking endless rows of Pursley's sodding podded peas for nothing! I will have to kill myself. Errrrrghhhhh, arghhhhhhh . . . Goodbye sweet world.

PS. Make sure you cry buckets at my funeral.

PPS. And make sure Scott Malone gets to hear about my early death so that he will realise what he missed.

Cinnamongirl: I am so sorry. It is all Dad's fault. I totally hate him for ruining everything. I have tried everything to make him understand. Begged, pleaded, got down on my knees, but he's not budging an inch. So I

	have tried and I am sorry. Really, really. I will make it up to you somehow. Maybe Christmas? Or half-term?
Irishbrat4eva:	Sorry? Christmas? Christmas is, like, a million years away. I am starting to reconsider the ending it all thing though. I have looked death in the eye and we had a chat and were both wondering if maybe there isn't some solution or alternative to you going to Greece. I seriously hope that there is cos having considered my kill-myself options, it's not looking like my best idea to date. The only gun I can find is Mark's plastic water pistol. All Mum's knives are blunt, and there's little else in the kitchen unless I stab myself with a soup ladle. And I've been through the medicine cupboard for pills and all I could find was a tube of Grandad's bunion ointment. Death by bunion ointment just doesn't sound poetic, does it? I'd die of embarrassment at the eulogy when the vicar reads out the cause of death (which would be difficult cos I'd be dead already and I guess you can't be double dead, or can you?) So. India Jane, you're just going to have to do something. Get me?
Cinnamongirl:	I do. I will. I am thinking about it.
Irishbrat4eva:	And so am I. Have discovered new death method though. Death by Chocolate cake. Yum yum chomp chomp . . .

Cinnamongirl:	Stop talking about dying, even if you are joking. It's doing my head in. Killing yourself is a crap idea – you might get trapped in some in-between world for all of eternity and you'd have no body any more. You could sing that song though – 'I ain't got nobody' – only you'd leave a gap between 'no' and 'body', so it would be 'I ain't got no body', if you get me.
Irishbrat4eva:	Hhm. Clearly this crisis has caused you to lose your mind. OK. Will stop eating the cake as I do feel kinda sick.

Fifteen messages back and forth later and Erin and I had agreed that Greece just wasn't an option and, between us, we devised a list of alternatives that Mum and Dad just might buy.

There was hope.

Plan A was my eldest brother Ethan, and I was straight round there the next morning.

'Please, Ethan. I'll babysit for the rest of the year,' I begged as Eleanor put her breakfast bowl on her head and oat and banana mush dripped down her face, 'if you let me stay with you.'

Jessica was out at the shops and poor Ethan looked stressed out of his mind as we watched the twins rub their breakfast into their hair. (Lara had taken one look at Eleanor and the mush on her head trick, clearly thought it was an excellent idea and done

45

the same.) Ethan indicated the overcrowded space he called home. 'I'm so sorry, India J,' he said, 'it's going to be a push as it is having Dylan for that one week. We just don't have the room. You can see that, can't you?'

Sadly, I could. He, Jessica and the twins lived in a two-bedroom terraced house in West Hampstead. Every square inch was jam-packed. Just getting through the hall earlier was a major achievement – I had to step over the twins' double buggy, Ethan's bike, bicycle helmets and economy packs of nappies and baby supplies. Even the living area felt cramped with books, magazines, and more supermarket bulk buys. I could see that there would be no space for me unless I slept under the table.

I didn't push it. Ethan looked like he needed a good night's sleep and I didn't want to put more pressure on him than he already had.

Plan B was Lewis. I called him but his answering machine was on and his mobile switched off. I glanced at my watch. Half past twelve. Knowing Lewis and weekend mornings from when he lived with us, he'd still be in bed.

I caught the tube and a bus up to his studio flat in Crouch End and, true to form, when he finally answered the door after several rings, he looked sleepy-eyed and his wavy dark hair was sticking out all over the place.

On the way upstairs, I quickly filled him in on why I was there but, once we got to the first floor and into the flat, one sniff of the room that he shared with his mate Chaz told me that I wouldn't last a day there, never mind a week. It stank of old fags, old beer and Indian takeaways. The curtains were still closed and, when I switched the light on, their living area was a mass of overflowing ashtrays, takeaway cartons and empty lager cans.

I washed up for him while he showered and got dressed then I told him my story.

'Sorry, sis, but no can do,' he said as he donned an old T-shirt from the floor. 'Anyway, you'll probably have a great time in Greece. Imagine. All that sun, sea. Be fab.'

'So you and Chaz go and let me stay here,' I said, thinking that if I was on my own in his flat at least I could keep it clean.

'You know they'd never allow it,' he said.

I did. Even my liberal parents weren't that liberal.

When I got home later that afternoon, I could hear the sound of doors slamming and someone cursing as soon as I stepped into the hallway where Dylan was sitting on the floor with about twenty pairs of shoes in front of him.

'What are you doing?' I asked.

'Shoe polishing. Got any to be done?'

I shook my head as a female voice up above let out a curse.

Dylan jerked his chin up towards the ceiling. 'Kate,' he said.

'Something happened?'

Dylan shrugged. 'Aunt Sarah called earlier but it's probably PMT.'

'Like you'd know.'

'I read,' he said.

'Have you ever thought of reading something normal for your age? Like a horror book or *Harry Potter* or something?'

'I need to know these things if I'm going to be a doctor,' said Dylan.

'Thought you were going to be an archaeologist.'

'That was last week. You feeling better about going to Greece?'

'No,' I said. 'Like you care.'

'Actually I do,' he replied. 'Least you won't be on your own out there any more.'

'Why? You coming now?'

'Nope,' said Dylan, then jerked his chin towards the ceiling again to where the sound of angry stomping and crashing continued.

'Kate?' I asked.

Dylan nodded.

'How come?'

'Her dad's got to go to the States on business or something so she can't go and stay with him, plus Aunt Sarah found out she hadn't been home last night.'

'Ah.'

'So that makes two sulky teenagers on route to Greece,' said Dylan.

I raced up the stairs to Kate's room where she had stopped

crashing about and had lit up a cigarette. 'You heard then?' she asked.

I nodded and crossed her room to open the window.

'You don't need to do that,' she said. 'Mum's not here and I wouldn't care if she was.'

I sat on the end of her bed as she puffed away on her cigarette.

'I'm not going,' said Kate. 'They can't make us. And anyway, it's probably a non-starter – I doubt they'll be able to get flights at such short notice. And if they do, we'll stage a sit-in. Protest. Go on a hunger strike. There's no way I am going out to holier-than-thou-land for a crap summer. No way.'

Great, I thought. 'Me neither,' I said.

Chapter 6

Take Off

'Flight B345 to Greece is now boarding at Gate 23,' came the announcement over the tannoy.

It was six in the morning. Aunt Sarah had managed to get some last minute flights, which had meant getting up at what felt like an ungodly hour. Neither Kate nor I were in a very good mood.

Mum was about to set off towards the gate. 'Right, girls,' she said as she beckoned us forward. 'Let's go.'

'We'll be fine from here,' said Kate through gritted teeth. 'We're not going to do a runner at this point in the game.'

Mum ignored her. 'Now, let's go through it all again. Tickets?'

Kate rolled her eyes, but I nodded. 'Yep. And I've got my passport and my boarding pass. You can go. We'll be fine.'

Mum began fishing in her bag. 'In a minute,' she said, then thrust a couple of cartons of vanilla yogurt towards us. 'I brought these for you for the journey.'

'No thanks,' said Kate. 'I don't do yogurt.'

'You take them, India Jane. I know you like vanilla.'

'There will be food on the plane, Mum, and in Greece,' I said. 'Especially yogurt.'

'Just in case there's nothing you fancy on the plane,' said Mum and pushed the cartons into my bag. 'Now, anything else?'

'We'll be OK from here,' I said. 'You can go.'

Mum stopped and glanced at her watch. 'OK, if you really think so.' Suddenly her eyes filled with tears. 'You sure you're going to be OK?'

'Like it would make a difference if I said no,' I said. I still felt angry that I was being sent off like an unwanted dog being confined to a kennel and all for *Dad's* convenience. He couldn't even be bothered to come with us to the airport. He had taken off this morning with a cheery wave goodbye to go to a meeting with his new orchestra. That was all he cared about now. I don't think he'd even noticed how mad I was with him this last week. He was too wrapped up in his latest venture to notice anyone or anything else.

Mum wrapped her arms around me and gave me a hug. She smelled lovely, of roses and lemons. 'Call as soon as you get there and e-mail regularly. Sarah's got broadband so it won't be a problem.' She hugged Kate too. 'Give your mum my love.'

'Yeah, right,' said Kate. 'Bye Aunt Fleur.'

'And look after my baby,' said Mum.

'Mu-*um*,' I groaned. 'Just go.'

'And remember your sun screen . . .'

This time I rolled my eyes although I was feeling wobbly inside about leaving my family behind. It so wasn't fair.

Mum took a deep breath, gave me a sad look then turned on her heel and went. For a brief moment, I felt like sitting on the floor and having a good blub, but Kate had taken off in the direction of our departure gate and I didn't want be left behind.

'Ridiculous,' she muttered when I caught up with her. 'First your mum, then an escort on the flight. What do they think we are, a pair of convicts? In fact I wouldn't put it past my mother to have arranged for us to be handcuffed into our seats.'

I was about to ask her what she meant about an escort for the flight when I spotted two policemen standing outside a duty free shop.

'Ah yes, there are our escorts now,' I said as we passed them.

Kate almost smiled, which would have been a first that week. She'd actually managed to out-sulk me. Not that anyone took much notice of either of us – plans for our trip went into full swing despite all our objections. And Kate's hunger protest only lasted half a day. 'Why should I impose suffering on myself when everyone else on this planet is already doing such a good job,' she said as she made both of us a cheese toastie on the evening of the first day of her fast.

When we got to our gate, people were sitting about waiting to be called to board so we found a couple of seats and sat down with them. Kate pulled out her phone and got busy texting her mates. I was about to do the same to Erin when I noticed a boy in jeans and a black T-shirt with a rucksack slung over his shoulder enter the waiting area. My breath caught in my throat.

'Ohmigod,' I gasped and Kate glanced up and over to where I was staring at Joe.

'Oh, him,' she shrugged. 'Yeah. Mum said he'd be on our flight when I spoke to her last night. I was about to tell you. Can you believe it? *He's* the escort. My mum asked his mum to tell him to keep an eye on us. Joe Donahue. As if!' She went back to her texting for a minute, then glanced up at me. 'Sorry I didn't tell you before. I forgot you fancied him.'

I felt myself blush. 'I so do not.'

Kate laughed. 'Whatever,' she said. 'He may be a few months older than me but if he tries to play the prefect for even one second, I'll tell him where he can stuff it.'

I glanced over at Joe. Somehow, I couldn't see him playing the head boy or chaperone even if he'd been asked to. He hadn't seen us or if he had, he wasn't acknowledging the fact. He made his way over to a row of seats in front of Kate and me and sat down away from us, facing out towards the runways and the planes. I liked the look of him even from behind – the way his hair curled up at the back of his neck, his broad shoulders, nicely toned arms, not too muscular but not puny either . . . Then I remembered what Kate had said about him being bad news with a trail of broken hearts behind him. I made myself look away and resolved to be cool if I saw him when we were on board.

As Kate continued with her texting, I noticed a couple of boys enter the area and clock Kate. They looked about eighteen; one was tall and slim with dark spiked-up hair, the other was fair with a heavier build like a rugby player. The fair one nudged the other as they walked past us and took the seats to our left. The dark-haired guy couldn't tear his eyes away from Kate's legs (she was wearing a tiny denim mini with peep-toe navy espadrilles with high wedges which made her legs look longer than ever).

She saw the boy looking and gave him a brilliant withering look. 'Seen enough or would you like me to hitch my skirt up some more?' she asked.

The boy wasn't put off at all and grinned back cheekily. 'Oh, some more, I think,' he said in a posh voice. 'You've got crackingly good legs.'

He said it with such enthusiasm that Kate couldn't help but break a smile, although she quickly made her face go disdainful again.

His mate leaned over. 'Deffo,' he said. 'I'd agree with Tom. Good legs.'

Kate raised an eyebrow, then turned away as if dismissing them. She was really good at being cool and I resolved to practise the 'one eyebrow up' look as soon as I next got in front of a mirror.

'So, where are you going?' asked the blond boy.

Kate glanced up at the sign about the gate. 'Duh,' she said.

'Oh right,' said the boy. 'Obvi. Yes. Of course. Stupid question. Greece.' He didn't seem very embarrassed though. 'I'm Robin.'

'And I'm Tom,' said his better-looking mate.

'And *I* am not interested,' said Kate.

Tom looked over at me.

'And neither is she,' said Kate. 'Want a Coke, India Jane?'

'India Jane,' said Tom. 'I'd like a Coke.'

'I wasn't asking you,' said Kate. 'Ignore them, India Jane.'

Robin reached over and hauled his travel bag on to his knee and lifted the lid so that Kate and I could see inside. 'Got some of this to put in it,' he said as he slightly lifted what looked like a bottle of vodka.

Kate did the one eyebrow raise again but this time looked into the boy's eye in a smiley kind of way as if to say she approved.

'Couple of Cokes coming up,' she said. 'Got some change, India?'

I nodded. Mum had given me some spare change before we left the house. I got up to go over to the machine to get the Cokes and although I didn't like suddenly being treated as Kate's private slave, I wasn't too bothered. Even though the boys looked like fun, I was more interested in the boy sitting with his back to me a few rows away. I figured that, if I got the Cokes, I could walk down his row on the way back and hopefully he'd notice me and say something.

I got the Cokes and walked towards Joe. He seemed to be engrossed in a magazine and I could see by the little white earphones that he was also listening to an iPod. I also noticed that he was wearing a pair of Converse All Stars. Black pin-striped ones. Cool. I walked as close as I could but he still didn't look up. I walked past and was about to go back to my place with Kate when I heard his voice.

'Excuse me . . .'

I turned around ready to do the 'one eyebrow up' cool look, but, not having had time to practise it, I think both eyebrows went up making me look like I'd just had a fright.

'Oh, it's you!' said Joe.

'Was last time I looked,' I replied, thinking I'd made quite a clever answer.

Joe looked distinctly underwhelmed. He pointed to my bag. 'Er . . . I think you're dripping something?'

'Drippi-*uh*?' I trailed off as I looked to where he was pointing. Oh. My. God. There was a trail of white gloop all along the aisle behind me. There were *spots* of it on my jeans. It seemed to be coming from my bag. I looked inside. One of the vanilla yogurts had burst and gone all over everything and was leaking out of the corner of the bag. 'Oh *nooooooooooooooo . . .*'

Joe was watching me with the same amused look that he'd had on his face in the chemist's on the day that I'd first seen him.

I scanned my brain for something earth-shatteringly brilliant and witty to say as I pulled out the yogurt carton and held it up in front of him. 'Yogurt. It's the one with friendly bacteria. Um. Those darn bacteria! They're so friendly they follow me everywhere.'

Joe smiled weakly and raised one eyebrow perfectly. (He must have been to the same 'learn to communicate with your eyebrows' morse code training school as Kate.) Then he went back to reading his magazine.

So much for my new cool image, I thought as I sloped off towards the nearest Ladies. I was about as cool as a tandoori curry with double chilli.

'There are the most amazing deserted beaches to skinny dip on,' said Kate as we got up to board the plane. 'I'll show you guys one night.'

She was like a different girl by the time our flight was finally called and Robin and Tom were her long-lost best buddies. As I'd witnessed all week, Kate could have won an Oscar for her sulky princess act, but, clearly from the way she was throwing her head back, her guffaws of laughter and her animated body language, she could change her mind on a whim, decide to make the best of things and be party animal supreme.

I have a lot to learn from her, I thought as I trudged behind her and the boys across the tarmac and up the steps to the plane. *I ought to do the same. There's nothing I can do to change the situation, so why be miserable? The only person to suffer will be me, so I may as well be positive.*

We found our places on board and settled down for the flight, and I resolved to do my best to have a good time in Greece, starting by making some new friends. Not that I could do much from where I was. I'd got the window seat, Kate was in the middle and Joe had been given the aisle. *Never mind,* I thought, *there will be time.* As the plane took off and soared into the sky, my head was full of images of Joe and me swimming in the waves. Kate and me barbecuing fresh fish caught by the boys. Robin and Tom driving Kate and me around in an open-topped jeep. And back to more swimming with Joe. Getting out of the sea with Joe. Sitting under the stars . . . Hhhm. I could get quite carried away if I let myself. So Joe was a heartbreaker. So what? He just hadn't met the right girl yet.

'Do you mind swapping with me?' Kate asked Joe as soon as the *Fasten your seatbelt* sign had been switched off and people began to move around the plane. 'I prefer an aisle seat.'

'Sure. Go ahead,' he said, and he got up, let her out and then they swapped seats. She gave me the most appallingly indiscreet wink as Joe settled next to me and I prayed that he hadn't seen her. Although I wanted to get to know him better and I definitely wanted him on my list of new best buddies, I didn't want it *yet*. The plane was hot. I was hot and I could distinctly smell something that resembled sour milk – and it was coming from my jeans and my bag. I'd applied some of my cinnamon perfume as well as trying to sponge off the spilled yogurt in the loo near the departure gate lounge, but it had sunk right into the fabric of both and needed a good soak before it was going to come out completely. I thought about making a joke about it, like *eau de* sour milk? It's the latest pong you know, but I decided against it – Joe hadn't exactly collapsed laughing at my friendly bacteria line. He gave me a brief smile and asked, 'All right?' as he settled in next to me then began to scan the in-house entertainment brochure from the seat pocket in front of him.

Tom and Robin were seated ahead of us and, when someone moved and left an empty seat next to them, Kate moved to join them and soon I could hear them chatting away and making plans for when they got to Greece. I was about to say something to Joe, but he put on his complimentary headphones and looked like he was about to settle in for a movie. I glanced through what was on offer, but I'd seen them all. I took another peek at Joe, but he looked immersed already and I didn't want to disturb his viewing. *Oh, this is a great start,* I thought as I looked out the window to see a landscape of white woolly clouds stretching out to the horizon in front of me. *Sky to the right. Boy watching movie to my left. Yargh, I'm trapped,* I thought as a feeling of claustrophobia came over me. Sometimes that happens to me on flights and the only way to get over it is to keep myself distracted. I could see that the opening credits had just begun to roll on Joe's screen so I quickly nudged him.

'Hey, do you mind if I take the aisle seat so I can move around?' I asked. 'I promise I won't disturb you again.'

Joe shrugged. 'Whatever,' he said, and he got up again so that I could move over. As I squeezed past him, he leaned into the back of my neck and inhaled. 'Hhm. You smell good.'

I blushed as I sat down. 'It's a perfume that my mum makes for me. Um. It's got cinnamon in it . . . and other things . . .'

'Yeah. Spicy,' he said. 'Unusual but nice.'

Phew, I thought, *so hopefully he can't smell the spilled yogurt.*

'Smell is our most potent sense, did you know that?'

'Er . . . no,' I replied and quickly scanned my brain for something interesting to say. My mind went blank and, a few moments later, Joe picked up his headphones again and seemed to lose interest.

As soon as he was immersed in his movie, a million things that I could have said flooded into my mind. I knew *loads* about making scent from watching Mum – how there are three notes: base, middle and light. How perfumers try and get a balance between the three. How they use flowers, herbs, wood, fruit. *Blooming bananas,* I thought. *I could have chatted for hours. What is the matter with me?* I thought about turning back to him and getting the conversation going again, but he was focused on his film. Instead I leaned forward to try and join in with Robin,

Tom and Kate in front. Back in the airport lounge, Robin had given me a 'vibe' and, even though he wasn't my type (I like boys with finer features and Robin has one of those full faces with bushy eyebrows and a big rubbery mouth), I thought that if Joe saw that he was interested in me, he might be a little jealous. Maybe.

And so I flirted. I laughed at Robin's appalling jokes. I even sat on his chair arm at one point, and when I was sure none of the air stewards were looking, I swigged back some vodka when he offered me the bottle. I would show Joe that I could be bad too. He glanced up when I swigged the bottle back, so I gave him a look which was meant to be cool and sophisticated, like 'tralah, I do this sort of thing every day. I am such an experienced woman of the world'. However, at that moment, the plane must have hit an air pocket because it lurched and I lost my balance, fell off the chair arm and was thrown backwards into the lap of a bald old priest in the middle seats. He didn't look too pleased to find a teenage girl sitting on his knee and neither did the elderly nun sitting next to him. I scrabbled up as fast as I could. Kate, Robin and Tom all had their backs to me and suddenly seemed intent on looking out of the window, but I could see by the way that their shoulders were shaking that they were having a right laugh.

Kate glanced back at me and gave me the thumbs up. 'Nice one, India,' she said.

I glanced over at Joe in the hope that he was still engrossed in his movie, but, no, he had witnessed me doing my prat act again. I shrugged my shoulders at him as if to say, 'What can you do? Not my fault.' He just rolled his eyes, smiled, shook his head and went back to his movie. A second later, the *Fasten your seatbelt* sign came back on and everyone was asked to go back to their seats, so I had to sit back down next to him.

I am going to pretend that I am not here, I thought as I fastened my seatbelt and closed my eyes. *Maybe that way I won't do anything to make a total idiot of myself.*

Not that Joe was at all interested in what I was doing. After his movie finished, he finally turned to me. 'Sorry I'm not being Mr Sociable,' he said. 'Had a few late nights lately so I'm going to have a kip.'

'S'OK. Me too,' I lied. 'Yes. Late nights . . .'

He gave me a look which was a cross between amusement and like he was trying to figure me out and then he fell asleep. He slept through the in-flight meal (chicken, stewed broccoli, dried up rice, a stale roll and a piece of chocolate fudge cake that tasted of chemicals). He slept through more turbulence. *And* through the announcement that we'd be landing in fifteen minutes. At one point, he lolled over and his head leaned on my shoulder. He looked so cute, angelic really and he had long curly eyelashes. Sitting there in such close proximity to his face and his mouth, feeling his breath on my skin and catching his scent, light and lemony, his thigh against mine, made me feel strange – uncomfortable and cosy at the same time. And he had been right about our sense of smell being our most potent sense. I had to resist the urge to lean over and nibble his bottom lip. Instead I made myself close my eyes and tried to put any such thoughts out of my mind. Sadly though, a part of me had taken the idea and run with it. In my imagination, Joe and I spent the rest of the flight in an Oscar-winning snogerama.

He finally woke when the plane touched down in Skiathos and the passengers started clapping. *So much for my riveting company,* I thought as he opened his eyes, looked around as if he wasn't quite sure where he was and seemed taken aback to see me sitting next to him.

'Wow,' he said. 'I was just having the *weirdest* dream!'

I felt myself blush for a moment then told myself that no way could he have known what was going on in my head. Not unless he was a mind reader. All the same, I didn't dare ask him what he'd been dreaming about.

Chapter 7

Cloud Nine

'Ohmigod,' I said to my reflection in the mirror in the Ladies at Skiathos airport.

After we'd landed, I'd gone straight in there. I looked a right mess. My face, neck and chest were flushed bright pink. It was my own fault. I shouldn't have drunk the vodka. Alcohol always has the same effect and that is to turn me into a Belisha beacon. My mascara had run and somehow my hair had become squidged up on one side. No wonder Joe switched off big time. A red head, with a red face, who stank of vanilla, and who may or may not have had head lice. I think *I'd* have slept the whole journey if I'd been sitting next to me. There was only one thing for it, somehow I had to wow him with my scintillating conversation on the way to the centre and let him know that there was more to me than the scent of sour yogurt and an alarmingly ability to act like a twit. I brushed my hair, applied my brick-coloured lip-gloss and got ready to face the world (and Joe) again.

As soon as we had collected our luggage, we went through into the arrival area where Aunt Sarah came swooping down on us. As always, she looked stylish, dressed in a white linen shift dress and some beads that looked like they were made from nuts and seeds (but expensive nuts and seeds). I noticed that Kate popped some gum in her mouth and distanced herself from Robin and Tom.

Aunt Sarah however gave them a friendly wave.

'You *know* them?' asked Kate.

'Oh yes – at least I know Tom,' said Aunt Sarah. 'He's one of Stourton family. I know his parents. Nice people. They've got a house up on the north of the island. Fabulous place. They spent a bomb on it. All us Brits on the island tend to get to know each other sooner or later.'

'Hey, Mrs Rosen,' said Joe coming over to join us.

'Hi, Joe. You want a lift with us?'

Joe shook his head. 'I'm going into town first, sort out a few details.'

Aunt Sarah nodded like she knew what he was talking about. 'Fine,' she said.

I wanted to ask, what details? Where are you going? Already my imagination had conjured up some stunning long-legged, wild-haired, dark-eyed Greek girl who oozed sophistication. I felt so jealous even though I didn't even know if she existed. *How mad are you?* I asked myself as I followed Aunt Sarah out of the airport building.

'Tell Mum I'll get the bus up,' called Joe then he turned to me. 'Catch you later.'

'Ye-umpf,' I said. 'Ner . . . Yeah. Later.' *So much for impressing him with my scintillating conversation,* I thought. My body might have landed but my brain seemed to be still somewhere up in the sky.

'Yeah. Ye-umpf. Ner . . .' he repeated, then smiled his 'oh aren't you an odd little thing?' smile at me.

I think I scowled back at him because, for a moment before he took off, he gave me a strange look.

'Oh, me too,' said Kate suddenly. 'I need a few things in town. Hold up, Joe, I'll come with you.'

Aunt Sarah shook her head. 'Oh no, you don't,' she said. 'There will be time later for going into town. First me and you have to have a word. You go on, Joe.'

Kate grimaced, then saluted her mother. 'Prisoner 436 reporting for duty, sir,' she said.

Aunt Sarah's posture sagged slightly. Behind her, Robin and Tom waved at Kate; Tom pointed at his watch and then acted out drinking from a bottle.

Kate raised her right eyebrow the tiniest amount and gave the slightest nod to register that she had seen him, then she turned to her mother, linked her arm and gave her a half hug. 'OK, Mommie dearest, let's have a word. Have you missed me then?'

'Course. Always,' said Aunt Sarah, but she looked slightly suspicious of the sudden display of affection.

'Hey, Mum. Good job I was on the plane with India Jane,' said Kate. 'You should have seen her throwing herself at men. One of them was a priest too. Sitting on his knee at one point, she was.'

'I was *not . . .*' I began, but Kate grinned at me and so did Aunt Sarah. I hope she knew that Kate was joshing.

As we drove away from the airport, I felt my spirits start to rise. There wasn't a cloud in the sky and, as we left the boring area with half-built hotels and apartments behind us and headed out towards the coast, the scenery opened up and became prettier with pine forests on hills to the right and some lovely white houses covered in dark pink bougainvillea lining the road to the left. When we got our first glimpse of the sea sparkling down below in the distance, I got that lovely feeling I always get when I see the ocean – like, yahay, holidays! We drove on through a small town where I clocked some interesting-looking shops to check out later, then along the winding coastal road that led to the north of the island. Occasionally, I caught a glimpse of a white sandy beach and holidaymakers lying on sunloungers or playing in the sea.

Maybe it won't be so bad here after all, I thought as I texted Erin.

Wether is hRe, wish U wRe luvly. Muahahaha. IJX

After about half an hour, we came to a sign on the road that said *Cloud Nine* and an arrow pointing to a lane leading up into the hills. There, Aunt Sarah swung the jeep to the right and we drove through rows of villas behind whitewashed walls. I tried to see in but the walls were too high for a good nosey. We passed a restaurant up on a corner of the slope and, between the terrace and some trees, I could see the amazing view they had out over the coastline. *Cool place for a romantic meal,* I thought as my imagination blasted an image into my mind of Joe and me eating up there, gazing out, holding hands. *Shut up, shut up, shut up mind,* I told myself as we went on past a couple of shops with stands outside selling fruit, flips-flops, snorkels, flippers, beachwear and postcards. *Good place for supplies,* I noted. The road suddenly came to an end, and we drove through an open wooden gate into a pebbly car park and up to a white bungalow that opened out at the front to a veranda with a high-beamed ceiling. *Must be the reception area,* I thought as I spotted a long wooden desk inside.

'We're here,' said Aunt Sarah and she pulled up outside the steps leading up to the veranda.

'Velcome to ze prison camp,' grumbled Kate, getting out of the car and stretching.

I took a look around and could see beyond the reception that there were a number of white bungalows with blue shutters dotted on the hill below.

As we unloaded our cases from the boot, a very suntanned lady in a turquoise sarong and T-shirt came out with glasses of cold juice for us.

'Pomegranate,' she said, handing them to us. 'Welcome. Kate, good to see you again.'

'Mf,' Kate replied. 'Not my idea, I can tell you.'

'And this is my niece, India Jane,' said Aunt Sarah.

'Welcome to Cloud Nine, India Jane,' she said. 'I'm Charlotte Donahue. Call me Lottie, most people do.'

Donahue? Wow. She must be Joe's mum, I thought as she ushered us up the steps. She wasn't what I imagined at all. She was stick thin with a mass of frizzy, greying curly hair and twinkly blue eyes. Since Kate had told me that Joe had a reputation as a bad boy, I don't know why but somehow I'd imagined his mum to be strict and straight-looking, like an accountant who works in the city or something, someone to rebel against, anyway, but Lottie looked like she could be fun.

Behind a desk in the reception area was a beautiful smiling Indian girl with a silver stud through her right eyebrow and a ring through her bottom lip.

'Girls, this is Anisha,' said Lottie as the girl nodded at us.

She then looked back in the direction of the car. 'No Joe?' she asked.

'Went into town,' Aunt Sarah replied.

Lottie made a resigned face, then picked up a large envelope from the reception desk and handed it to me. 'Here, India Jane.

Take one of these. It's the welcome package that we give to all of our guests. It tells you what's happening when and where and a map of the centre. If you like, I'll show you round then take you to your room. You'll be sharing with Kate.'

'Oh Mu-*um*,' groaned Kate. 'Can't I at *least* have my own room?'

Aunt Sarah shook her head. 'All the singles were booked out ages ago, sweetheart. You know how popular they are. Anyhow, you'll be fine in with India Jane.'

Kate narrowed her eyes and tightened her mouth. *Any minute now, smoke's going to come out of her ears,* I thought. I felt hurt by her reaction to sharing with me.

Aunt Sarah gave her friend a weary look, then turned back to Kate. 'OK Kate, that's enough of the attitude. In fact, I think that you and I need to have that small word *now,*' she said and indicated that Kate should follow her. 'Lottie, can I hand India Jane over to you?'

Lottie nodded. 'Course you can. We'll take good care of her.'

Kate rolled her eyes at me, but did as she was told and stomped after her mother into a room that looked like an office to the left of the reception.

'Just you and me then,' said Lottie as her phone rang. 'Excuse me a mo.'

She took her call, then came back to me. 'Sorry, bit of an emergency in the kitchen. I'll have to show you around later. There's always something happening somewhere! Er . . .' She called to the girl behind the desk. 'Anisha, could you show India Jane her room? She's in Cloud Fifteen.'

'Hey, India Jane. Cool name. Welcome,' said Anisha, stepping out from behind the reception. 'Follow me.'

I picked up my bag and let her lead the way. She was barefoot, dressed in loose white trousers and a sleeveless T-shirt and her hair was pulled back into a simple ponytail, but there was something about her that was effortlessly stylish and elegant. I felt overdressed next to her in my red sneakers, pink T-shirt, red shirt and purple nail polish.

The compound was busy as we walked along the path that led to the sleeping quarters. We passed several huts where I could see various groups doing different classes: some doing t'ai chi on a grass verge, others painting, others dancing.

'How many people are there?' I asked.

'About sixty,' Anisha replied. 'There are twenty bungalows for accommodation, some for four sharing, some for two and a couple have single rooms in them.'

It didn't feel like there were so many rooms as we made our way along. The design of the place meant that the huts where people slept were away from the rest of the complex and were spaced at intervals down the slope, each with its own bougainvillea-covered veranda looking out over the coast and between them were the pine trees providing shade. *No wonder people come here,* I thought as I spotted a middle-aged man dozing in a hammock strung between two trunks. *It has a really peaceful vibe.*

'Early morning and late afternoon is activity time,' said Anisha, leading me past an open area between huts where a small group were practising yoga. 'If you look in your brochure, it tells you what's on when. Have you any idea what you'd like to do?'

'Not really. Maybe some art classes.'

'There are loads of those,' said Anisha. 'Morning and afternoon.'

When we reached a bungalow at the bottom of the slope, Anisha unlocked the blue door and let me in.

'I have to go back now,' she said with a smile. 'Let me know if you need anything.'

I put my bag down and looked around. It was a light, airy room with white walls, a high open-beamed roof and a parquet floor. It smelled clean, of polish, herbs and lemons. At one end were two single beds with sky blue covers and next to them were two bedside cabinets. To the left was a pine wardrobe, a shelf with a couple of paperbacks on it and a mirror above it. On the right was a wicker sofa with a bamboo and glass coffee table in front and on that a vase with a sprig of green in it. I picked up the vase and sniffed. Rosemary. I knew the scent from Mum's bath gel concoctions. *Nice but a bit impersonal,* I thought as I opened a door to the back which led to a small bathroom with a loo, shower and sink. *But then it is a sort of hotel, I can't expect it to look like Aunt Sarah's home back in London.*

Next, I checked out the front of the bungalow where there

was a narrow veranda with two wicker chairs on it. I sat down and looked out at the view. It was lovely. Sea and sky as far as the eye could see and it looked as if there was a bay behind some trees at the bottom of the slope.

Up until that moment, I hadn't given any thought to what it was going to be like once we got to the centre. I had been too busy objecting and then travelling, getting here. Suddenly, it felt anticlimactic. Like everything had been in motion and had suddenly stopped. The place was *so* quiet, peaceful, but I felt odd – like if I was still moving amidst the stillness. I was restless. Twitchy. I wished there was a TV or something I could flick on – some sound to fill the silence. A computer I could e-mail on. Some way I could have contact with the outside world. What was I supposed to do with myself now that I had arrived? Go and join in with the people back on the grass straining to get their legs up behind their necks. *Not today,* I thought. Although I can do it. Mum and Dad have practised yoga since forever and so Dylan and I did too. The 'Salute to the sun' was part of our daily ritual and, until I got to Ireland, I thought everyone sat in the lotus position when they sat on the floor. The way I could get myself into the strangest positions was one of the things that used to make Erin laugh.

I went inside and pulled my phone out of my bag to try and text Erin. No joy. The battery needed charging. Stupid me, I meant to do it before we'd left. *So. What to do?* I asked myself. I decided to put my phone on recharge, then began to put away the things I had brought for the trip.

Just as I'd finished, Kate burst in. *Phew,* I thought as she dumped her bag on the end of one of the beds. *Company.* She may not have liked the idea of sharing a room, but I was secretly pleased that I wasn't going to be alone. *Maybe she's got some idea of what we can do,* I thought as I lolled on my bed and watched her empty the contents of her suitcase on to hers, change her T-shirt, comb her hair back and don her shades.

Then she got up.

'See yus later,' she said and she picked up her straw bag and headed for the door.

'Later? Why? Where are you going? Can I come?' I asked. 'And are you going to leave all your stuff on the bed?'

Kate's expression registered irritation. 'India. We might be cousins. We might have to share a room, but we're not joined at the hip. OK?'

I felt as if someone had poured cold water over me and Kate must have seen my face fall because she let out a slow breath.

'Look,' she said with a sigh. 'I just need some space for a while. OK? Like, this is not my ideal summer and I need to readjust my head. Maybe you can come next time, OK?'

And then her phone went. She didn't even wait for my reaction. She was on her mobile and out the door.

Not my ideal summer either, I thought after she'd gone. *Not that anyone has asked what is.* I flicked through the two novels on the shelf, then put them back. One was a murder story and the other was a caring sharing self-help book. I wasn't in the mood for caring sharing, nor was I in the mood for reading.

I decided to go and have a wander around the site, so I donned my shades and set off back up towards the reception area where most of the classes seemed to be based.

There were the classes that I'd seen earlier, but all sorts of other stuff was going on too. There was a hut where a couple of people were learning massage, another where they seemed to be learning how to make jewellery, another where a group of five were singing or doing some sort of voice work (actually they sounded like they were being strangled). I passed a drumming class, a fencing group, a writing group and another hut where I think people were doing some kind of healing or therapy as a few people were crying on mats and others hugging them. In an adjacent hut, a couple of people were doing mad hippie dancing to some kind of droning groaning sound. *Not for me,* I thought as I moved quickly on. I passed a kitchen area which was busy with a group of people chopping and cutting vegetables. One of them waved but I darted out of her eye line in case I got roped in. Not that I minded helping out in the kitchen but didn't want to just yet. There were a couple of open huts on a terrace area where it looked like people could get drinks and snacks and there were a few people at a long table in the middle, talking and laughing. They seemed so at home, like they knew each other and they belonged there. There was no sign of Kate, Lottie or Aunt Sarah. Or Joe.

I got a bottle of water from the bar area and made my way

back down the slope to our bungalow. I let myself back into our room, lay on my bed and stared at the skylight in the sloped roof. There was the beginning of a cobweb up in the right-hand corner.

It felt *so* quiet.

Somewhere in the distance a dog barked. A fly buzzed at the window.

It was so quiet that you could almost *hear* the silence, but I guess that was the point. That was what people paid to come here for, but to me, after the hussle and bustle of London, it felt . . . *boring.*

How on earth am I going to get through four whole weeks here? I asked myself. I was in a place full of people, sixty of them, according to Anisha. *It's not like I'm alone,* I told myself. *So why do I feel so lonely?*

No one cares about me, I thought as I wondered what Mum and the boys were doing back in London. Tears pricked my eyes. I felt cross with Kate. She'd made me feel like I was a hanger-on. A clingy hanger-on. *This is all new to me and I didn't exactly ask to come here either. She could have been more sensitive.*

I took my phone off the recharger and texted Erin.

WethR is luvly. rly *rly* rly rly wsh U wre hre.

Chapter 8

Exploring

'Sorry about yesterday,' said Kate the next morning. 'Let's go and get some brekkie and I'll show you what to avoid.'

'It's OK. I'll be fine,' I said. 'You don't have to.'

Kate raised an eyebrow. 'Ah. I'm in the doghouse. Understandable. I am a cow. Hmm. A cow in the doghouse? Hmm.' She got down on her knees and put her palms together. 'I, Kate, do beg your forgiveness. Please let me make it up to you today or my soul shall be tossed into a cesspool of pig poo and I shall be tormented forever.'

I couldn't stay mad at her for long, so I smiled back at her. 'Thou art forgiven, oh cow girl in the doghouse in pig poo. But really, Kate, if you want to go off on your own then do. I'm cool,' I said. Although I wanted to hang out with her, no way did I want to follow her round if I wasn't wanted.

Kate got up off the floor and sat back on her bed. 'I know you're cool. It's just . . . I dunno, I get mad with my mum sometimes and have to get away and get my head together. It's, like, one day she's all concerned mother and where have I been and who with and what doing? And then she's so busy with all her businesses, she hardly notices that I exist.'

'Tell me about it,' I said. 'She sounds like my dad lately. In fact, I think he only liked me when I was little and cute and used to follow him around everywhere. Now I've grown up, I'm not sure he even likes me any more.'

Kate nodded. 'Yeah. Like, sometimes I just wish Mum'd be consistent so that I knew what to expect. Do you get me? Anyway. Boring me stuff. Yada yada yada yawn. So. OK, plan is, humour Mommie dearest and then get the hell out of this loserville as fast as possible. I mean, have you seen some of the saddos and what they get up to?' She went into a great mimic of some of the people doing the strange singing I'd witnessed yesterday. 'I mean, get a life. Someone tried to give me a hug yesterday in the snack bar. Like, ee-ew, I thought. Do I know you? Do I, like, want to *hug* you? A lot of touchie-feelie spewie stuff goes on here and, quite honestly, it makes me want to hurl.'

I had to laugh. 'Aw and I was going to ask you for a hug too. Come on, Kate, you have learn to share and care.'

'Back off, lezzer,' said Kate with a grin. 'Only people I hug are fit boys and even they have to earn it. So, how do you fancy grabbing a bite of brekkie, then we head down to town and the beach? I've OK'd it with Mum. She thinks you ought to get a feel of where you are and see some of the surrounding locations.'

'Really? Great. Cool,' I said. I felt relieved that I'd have someone to hang out with and go to the food area with, after last night's supper. Aunt Sarah had collected me, early evening, to go to eat with her and a bunch of people on the main long table. They all clearly knew each other well and, although I tried to join in, I couldn't help feeling like the odd person out. Like I was standing outside myself, watching myself, wondering where or how I could fit in. A tall thin guy with dark hair in a pony tail was serving food and seemed to notice my discomfort. He looked about Kate's age and gave me a friendly smile and introduced himself as Liam Payne. He asked if I wanted to join him and his group on their table after supper. I shook my head and hoped that I didn't appear unfriendly. It was just that the group he pointed out, like everyone else there, seemed overly cheerful and at home. I wasn't in the right mood for meeting a whole crowd of new people just yet. I looked around for Joe and spotted him on a table with his mum and he gave me a brief smile but no indication that he was going to come over to me or would like me to go over to him and why should he? I asked myself. He probably thought I was OK with Aunt Sarah and her lot. Plus, I still felt a little embarrassed about the mega snog fantasy I'd had about him on the plane. I decided to be really cool with him for the rest of the stay and, after dinner, went straight back to my room and had an early night. I fell asleep in an instant and was only vaguely aware of Kate coming in at some time past midnight.

At breakfast, after we'd got our food from the buffet (muesli for me, croissants and raspberry jam for Kate), we found a table in the corner of the terrace from where we could see all the 'inmates' as Kate called them. The sun was beaming down and there was a gentle breeze and it did feel good to be there. Kate began a running commentary about who everyone was and why they were there. It was totally made up, at least I *think* it was.

'Over there are the lesbian librarians from Clipping Horton: Mavis and Maureen,' said Kate, giving a wave to two elderly women in matching lilac kaftans. 'Sisters. They only came out as gay in their fifties to the amazement of their husbands, seventeen children, forty grandchildren and twenty cats. The cats were the most shocked of all. I don't know if you know this or not, but some cats can be quite narrow minded about sexuality . . .'

'I know,' I said with a heavy sigh. 'It's very hard being a gay cat, in fact a lot of them choose not to tell at all. Our big black cat Boris, in Ireland, was gay and had to have cat counselling before he came out.'

Kate gave me a big smile. 'Good for Boris,' she said. 'And

good for you. You're quite clearly as barmy as I am! Anyway, M and M come to the island each year to make erotic sculptures of fertility goddesses to sell in the café of their local library when they go back. Next to them, is oh . . . Liam Payne.' She did a mock shudder. 'He gives me the creeps.'

She was looking at the boy who had been friendly last night when he was serving supper. I had intended to go and talk to him today and explain why I didn't take up his offer to join his group. 'Why?'

Kate shrugged. 'Um . . . too touchy feely. He was here the first time I came. He's into the whole spiritual trip, but . . . I don't know, there's just something that I don't like about him. He's so intense, like he doesn't just hug, like, you know, a friendly hug – you hug, you let go. He *hugs* like it's some healing emotionally-charged moment that's loaded with meaning. Like he holds on too long until I want to push him off with great force.'

I laughed and glanced back at Liam. He looked OK to me and he was the only person last night who had seemed to have picked up on the fact that I felt left out. He was talking to Anisha and another girl dressed in white with a long plait down her back and a white dot in-between her eyebrows. He saw me looking and smiled. I smiled back but decided not to go and talk to him, at least not while Kate was looking on. I was about to ask more about Liam, but she launched back into her commentary and I didn't want to interrupt when she was so clearly on a roll.

'Now . . . the bald man with the paunch, in the long shorts and socks and sandals, in the far corner? Hhmm, what an attractive look. Not. Now he used to be a playboy porn star until, one morning, he had a vision. Not unlike that what-his-name St Paul on the road to Damascus. Well, our chap, he saw the light on the North Circular, just behind the World of Leather, and hasn't been the same since. Actually, the light he saw was the lasers from Wembley stadium, but no one liked to tell him and shatter his fantasy. Anyhow, he's here to get in touch with his inner nerd, which so far he's doing rather well at. And see that lady over there in the sarong and tank top with the big belly? Her story is that she was bored in her office job one day and, in her coffee break, she discovered that she could make amazing patterns with her fat tummy. She developed her skill into a kind of flab origami. Now she teaches classes in it. It's all the latest rage in certain parts of California. The group of ladies on the back table? What a bunch they are! Alcoholics. Drug addicts. Nicotine addicts. They are here to deal with their various addictions and are doing a workshop called 'Kick Your Crutch in Skiathos.'

When she said that, I laughed so hard that I spat out my muesli and of course it had to be just when Joe was walking past. An oat flake flew out and stuck to his upper left arm.

Oh nooooooooooooooooooo, I thought as he gave us the briefest nod. He was looking really cool in black jeans and a grey T-shirt with the Superman logo on the front. I hoped that he hadn't noticed the flake but, after he'd gone past a few feet, without even looking down, he flicked the flake off with the forefinger of his right hand. *Oh double noooooooooooooo*, I thought. *Why do I always have to act the village idiot when he makes an appearance?*

'Does he always keep to himself?' I asked, watching him go to the table with yogurts and fresh fruit.

Kate followed my gaze. 'Who? Joe? Dunno,' she said. 'I know he's been here a few times but never at the same time as me before. Back in London, he's quite the party boy though. I heard Mum and Lottie talking about him. He wants to go to art college after school apparently. Mum said he's signed up to do some of the art classes here, that is when he's not working.'

Oh no, no, noooooooooo, I thought, *that's it then. No way can I go and do those classes now. If I did, he'd think I was doing them because he was. Annoying, annoying.*

'Hey,' said Kate. 'Why don't you show him some of your paintings when we get back to London? You could do the 'come up and see my etchings' line and, he will be so impressed, he'll fall at your feet in worship.'

'You've changed your tune. Back in London, you warned me off him.'

Kate laughed. 'I know but, let's face it, bad boys have their appeal. I could see on the way over here that you really do like him and I would never stand in the way of true love.'

'True love? Yeah, right,' I said. 'No chance. Somehow I think Joe has made up his mind about me.'

'Which is?'

'That I am too young, too stupid, too . . .' I made my eyes go cross-eyed and my mouth go squiffy. My best zombie look. 'I don't know.'

Of course this was at the exact moment that Joe sat at the end of the table and glanced over at me. I straightened my face and gave him a weak smile. He smiled back, but I could tell what he was thinking and that was: that girl is totally bananas. Queen of the whole fruit bowl in fact.

Kate leaned over. 'So change his mind,' she whispered.

'Nah,' I said. 'Not really interested. Not really my type.'

Kate laughed. 'Which is why you went pink when he walked past and why you can't stop looking at him.'

'Kate.'

'Yeah.'

'Shut up.'

She laughed again, but she did shut up and finish her croissant.

After breakfast, we dropped in to see Aunt Sarah in her office, then we caught the shuttle bus from the car park outside reception into the town that we'd driven through the day before. *This is more like it,* I thought as we cruised the shops in the narrow lanes there and tried on sunglasses, sniffed all the scented candles and tried on jewellery and sandals. I bought a sleeveless white T-shirt like Anisha's, a pair of white cotton trousers and some postcards and Kate bought an ankle bracelet.

Then we went to one of the many cafés lining the front where some stunning yachts and boats were anchored. We ordered *café lattes* and sat back to enjoy the sun and the view. It was a great place to people watch – all sorts of shapes and sizes strolled past, while others pottered and posed on the boats moored in the harbour.

Once again, Kate gave me her take on the people who went past, who they were and why. '. . . The tall man who looks like a giraffe. Now, he's on holiday with his new wife.' (Clearly it was his mother.) 'Sadly she stayed too long in the sun last year and smoked too many cigarettes and has prematurely aged. He won't mind, though, because he's with her for her money. That little girl over there in the red shorts?' (She pointed to a man and his small daughter.) 'She looks about eight? Wrong. She's sixty-four. Got carried away having face lifts and plastic surgery. Sad really, some people just don't know when to stop. And here comes Mr and Mrs Wide-eyed Sweetie. They're just married. On honeymoon. He has yet to discover that she is a man and, although now called Betty, she used to be Keith.'

As she continued her observations, I was laughing so hard that I didn't notice Tom and Robin creep up behind us. They joined us for coffees and Tom told me a little about the island and what there was to do there. Eat, swim and sunbathe seemed to be the main activities on offer. *All things I can do,* I thought, making a note of his recommendations of various cafés to try.

After our coffees, we walked back through the lanes to the

car park. Judging by the easy familiar way that Tom and Kate were being with each other and their linked arms, I could tell that, when she had disappeared yesterday, it had been to see him. Their relationship had clearly moved on a notch since we had all got off the plane. I walked along behind them with Robin and we went through the usual getting to know each other better stuff – like asking questions about schools and where we lived, what music we liked, what websites and so on.

'What's your star sign?' I asked.

'Virgo. You?'

'Gemini with Sagittarius rising.'

'Oh. You into all that stuff then?'

'I know a bit. Me and my mate Erin read up about it back in Ireland.'

He linked arms with me. 'So do Virgos and Geminis get on then?'

'Um. Yeah. Think so,' I lied – I seemed to remember that Virgo was an earth sign and Gemini was an air sign, so they weren't the most compatible.

'You got a boyfriend?'

'No. We only just moved to London,' I replied.

'What about back in Ireland before the move?'

'Nope. No one special.' I really hoped that he didn't think he was in with a chance with me because, on seeing him for a second time, it only confirmed that, though a nice enough guy, he so wasn't my type.

At the car park, we piled into their open-topped jeep and, with Tom driving, took off back along the coast road to a beach they knew on the west side of the island. I felt really glam sitting in the back of the jeep with my shades on and, once or twice, I saw people checking us out as we drove past. I had to get out my baseball cap to put on at one point because my hair was flying about so much that, I was sure that if I didn't, I was going to arrive at the beach with my hair sticking up like a troll. Not a great look.

The beach wasn't too busy and had a taverna at one end and sunloungers at the other. Tom paid a deckchair boy for some beds and we set about the serious business of sunbathing. It wouldn't be long before I looked as brown as one of the locals, because I inherited my father's olive skin which tans easily and doesn't burn. Tom and Kate slathered lotion all over each other and I could see that Robin had the same idea about applying some on to me and vice versa. When he asked, I did put some on his back and then quickly squirted some over myself and rubbed it in before he had a chance to offer. I think he got the message and didn't push it. As I lay back, watching people dip in and out of the sea, and felt the warmth of the sun of my skin, I began to feel relaxed for the first time in days.

At lunchtime, we padded along the sand to the taverna and had delicious feta cheese salads with fresh basil and tomatoes that tasted sweet and juicy. The boys and Kate drank beers and I had Coke. After lunch, as we strolled back to our sunloungers,

Tom picked up Kate, put her over his shoulder, then ran into the sea and threw her in. Robin looked over at me, but I was too quick for him and sprinted down the beach where I went in on my own. In my own time. I've never been one of those people who can dive right in. I have to do it stage by stage, unless it's the Indian ocean, which is like walking into a warm bath. The ocean here, however, was the Mediterranean and not warmed up yet (if it ever was). First I went in knee-deep, then hip-deep, then had a quick dip up to my shoulders. There were some undercurrents that were so cold it took my breath away. Robin came in after me. Straight in, but even he shrieked when he realised how cold it was. I took a really deep breath and ducked myself in properly. After a few seconds, it felt lovely and I swam out about fifty metres, then put my arms out, fell back and let myself float. I love doing that. It's one of the fabbest feelings in the world – the salt water keeping you up, a blue sky above. Heaven.

After our swim, we all had a doze in the sun. Then, Tom drove us back up to the centre where Aunt Sarah insisted he and Robin stay for supper with the rest of the guests.

'I'm so pleased that he and Kate have hooked up,' Aunt Sarah said to me when we went up to the buffet to get our meals. 'Ed and Marcia Stourton have had a place on the island for over twenty years and know all the right people here. Good family to keep in with and I think he'll be a good influence on her.'

I nodded and smiled, but I wasn't as sure that 'good influence' was the right description for Tom who had 'bad boy' written all over him. I decided not to share my opinion with Aunt Sarah nor tell Kate about how pleased her mother was that she was spending time with him. Knowing Kate, she'd dump him immediately just to annoy her.

'And how are you, India? Settled in OK?' asked Aunt Sarah.

I nodded again. I could honestly tell her that I was fine. *It's amazing how your experience of a place can change in just one day,* I thought, helping myself to roasted vegetables and couscous and going to sit with my new friends. It was so totally opposite to how lonely and strange I had felt last night. I only wished that Joe had been there so that he could see what a popular person I was, who made friends easily, but sadly he was nowhere to be seen.

Ah well, there's always tomorrow, I thought as I tucked into my supper.

Chapter 9

Idiot Me

As the week went by, Kate and I fell into an easy routine. Breakfast at the centre, have a laugh and make up stories about the 'inmates', then a catch-up with Aunt Sarah, who always seemed to be preoccupied with a million things to do. I began to understand how Kate felt about her – she did treat us as if we were on her list of things to do. Check daughter and niece still alive. Tick. Both present and correct. Is Kate's mobile charged so she's reachable wherever she is? Tick. And off she'd go on to the next item.

After breakfast, I'd tidy my side of the room that I shared with Kate. It was funny because it soon looked like there was an invisible line separating it into two halves. Mine was neat and tidy – not a thing out of place. Kate's half was a total mess. Her sheet was always thrown back and the bed was covered with stuff: her bag, her phone, clothes, nail polish, make-up, tissues, gum, chocolate bar wrappers. I offered to tidy up for her, but she did the raised eyebrow thing, pointed at my side and said, 'Your space,' then pointed to her side: 'My space.' I nodded. Understood.

Next, I'd e-mail Erin, Mum, Dad and the boys from the cyber room, which was adjacent to Aunt Sarah's office in reception. Not that it seemed that anyone apart from Erin could have cared less whether I kept in touch or not. Dad sent a hurried message one day. *Darling India, hope you're having fun. Busy busy. Dad. Pff to that,* I thought. Mum sent a slightly longer one but it didn't sound like she was missing me much either. Too busy busy too, having fun with Dad. Pff to her as well. Dylan sent an article about sun damage and the importance of protecting one's skin. He really is one weird twelve-year-old. There were no messages from Ethan or Lewis but that was to be expected. They were hopeless about keeping in touch and always had been. They even forgot birthdays. Only Erin sent regular messages. At least she seemed to be genuinely missing me.

After 'contact' with the outside world, it would be time for chores. Kate was really good at playing the good girl, chopping veggies for the lunch, preparing peppers for the evening meal, being little Miss Helpful. We even did a couple of the yoga classes to show extra willing, but we drew the line at hippie dancing or any of the healing schmealing ones.

'Got to play the game,' said Kate as she swept the dining terrace after breakfast one day. 'If I acted sulky the whole time, Mum would only get mad with me. So, I'm the model daughter part of the time and then, the rest of the time, I can do what I like.'

And she did too. I think her mum would have had a heart attack if she knew what she got up to. She drank vodka with Robin and Tom, smoked cigarettes until she stank of them, and I know she was considering having sex with Tom because, on the first Friday after we'd arrived on the island, I saw her buying condoms. She saw me looking at her in the shop and did her 'raised eyebrow' look. I knew what she meant. I was becoming fluent in eyebrow talk. She meant, 'You tell Mum and you're dead.'

They always offered me whatever they were having, but I usually said no because alcohol gave me a rash and a headache. Sometimes I felt like the immature, boring straight cousin that had been dumped on Kate because there was no one else to babysit me, but my only alternative was to hang out on my own up at the centre where most of the guests were middle-aged and I didn't want to do that. Sometimes, I had a drink just to show that I wasn't a total killjoy, but I didn't really enjoy it like they seemed to.

After breakfast on the first Saturday, Kate went to wash her hair, so I went to check out the art rooms and found Joe was in there working on something.

He looked up when I walked in. 'Hey,' he said. 'Haven't seen you around this week.'

'You neither.'

'Been working. Bar in town.'

'Oh right.' *So that's where he's been,* I thought.

'Yeah. Need to earn some dosh and it's something to do, you know.'

'Yeah. What you doing?' I asked, then I cursed myself. It was *obvious* what he was doing. 'I mean, clearly you're working, drawing, er, doing art. Sorry. I seem to be having an idiot attack. It's the sun. Makes me loopy. Oh shut up, India.'

Joe laughed and his eyes crinkled in a really lovely way that made him look even more attractive. 'Yes, the sun makes me loopy too. And yes, I am doing some art.'

'Can I look?' I asked.

'Er . . .' Joe hesitated. 'I guess. It's not finished yet.'

'I won't if you don't want. I hate people looking at my work before it's ready.'

'You paint or draw?'

I nodded. 'Both. Not very good . . .'

'Maybe I could see one day. You know, back in London?'

Yes! I thought and inwardly punched the air. *Result!*

'Are you doing some classes here?' he asked.

'I might,' I said. And then I spotted an amazing charcoal drawing on the desk to his right. It was of Lottie. 'Hey, did you do that?'

Joe glanced over at the drawing. 'That? Oh yeah. It's my mum.'

'I can see that,' I said and walked over to take a closer look. 'It's totally brilliant.'

For a second, Joe blushed slightly. 'Thanks. I'm trying to brush up my portraiture, you know for my portfolio. I don't usually do people, but it's good to have a variety of work for college interviews.'

'Well, you've really got an eye for it. You've caught your mum exactly. She looks . . . alive, like she has weight. You know how some drawings of people look like they're floating? Least, mine do – although I like doing people best. I find it hard to make people look like they have flesh, if you know what I mean.'

'I do,' said Joe, and he looked straight at me like he was sizing me up for a drawing. I felt myself blush because, when our eyes met, I got the lovely warm honey feeling in my stomach again like I'd felt on the first day I'd seen him. I glanced away.

'Umf, got to go now. Kate's washing her hair.'

'Kate? Oh right. She needs help?'

'No. Course not. In fact I don't know why I said that,' I said, thinking, *And I don't know why I told him that!*

And there it was again. The look of amusement on his face. 'Using that shampoo you bought in London, is she?'

'No. I told you. No head lice. Not in our family.'

'Just teasing, India Jane,' he said. 'Don't look so serious.'

'I . . . I . . . Me? Serious? Me. No . . . I'm a laugh a

minute . . .' *Leave now*, said a voice in my head. *You're going to start talking drivel*. 'OK. Super. Later.'

Super? I thought. *Who the hell says super!!*

'Later,' he said with a grin. 'Take it easy.'

'Yeah, later,' I said and cursed myself again. *Idiot, saying 'later' twice. He must think that I'm simple, And just when I'd managed to have a half decent conversation*, I thought, heading for the door. *Still, we have something in common. Art. I shall think up some wildly interesting things to say about it and impress his socks off.*

I spent the rest of the day down on the beach with Kate, Robin and Tom, thinking about what gems I could casually drop into the conversation the next time I saw Joe, but he wasn't around by the time we got back in the evening.

I stuck my head into the art room the next day after breakfast in the hope that he'd be there again but he wasn't. As Kate and I were going down to the town, I persuaded her to cruise by the bar where he worked, but he wasn't there either.

'Joe Donahue?' said a pretty dark-haired waitress behind the bar when Kate asked where he was. 'He did the early shift. You just missed him. Who shall I say stopped by?'

'Oh, no one,' I said.

'Kate and India Jane,' said Kate.

I punched her lightly on the arm as we left. 'I don't want him to think I'm following him around,' I whispered, then I noticed that the waitress was staring at us through the window. 'She's trying to work out who we are.'

Kate glanced back. 'Yeah. Knowing Joe, there's probably a stream of girls in there asking for him.'

'Really?'

Kate laughed. 'No. Only you. You *lurve* him.'

'I do not. I told you —'

'India! You *can* trust me. I won't blow your cover.'

Later that night, I spotted Joe back up at the centre at the buffet bar where people were queuing for supper.

He glanced around and noticed me standing behind him, so I took a deep breath and launched into the speech that I had prepared in my head. It was something that the art teacher at my last school had said and everyone had thought he was a really cool guy. Joe was bound to be well impressed and, in my mind, we would spend hours walking barefoot on the sand under the stars discussing life and art.

'I know many say that it's chocolate box art, but personally I like the Pre-Raphaelites, particularly Rossetti and Burne-Jones. I think that there's far too much snobbery when it comes to art. Too much intellectualism and one ought to go with one's gut.'

Joe looked at me as if I was talking gobbledegook. 'Er . . . pardon?'

I repeated my brilliant speech. 'I know many say that it's chocolate box art but personally I like the Pre-Raphaelites, particularly Rossetti and Burne-Jones. I think there's far too much snobbery when it comes to art. Too much intellectualism and one ought to go with one's gut.'

Joe burst out laughing. Then he made his face look very solemn. 'Wow. Yeah. Yes. Absolutely right. India Jane. Snobbery. Intellectualism. Quite correct. Now. Er . . . Thing is . . . whether to have the roasted veg or lentil bake? Hhmmm? Ought to go with my gut, you say?' He helped himself to the lentil bake. 'Right. See you then.' And off he went to sit on a table with his mother.

So much for my fantasy about walking along the sand – much better if I bury myself in it, I thought. I took some rice and beans and made a promise to myself to keep out of his way and keep my mouth shut for the rest of the holiday.

My vow proved to be easy to stick to, since most nights he took off on his own after supper and, although I was intrigued to know where he went, no way was I going to ask him. Part of me was disappointed by his lack of interest, but I wasn't going to put myself forward for any kind of rejection. I might act like an idiot in front of him, but I wasn't that stupid.

At least I still had Kate, Robin and Tom to hang out with and, in the second week, we went to a different beach each day and I began to feel less like a stranger on the island. Kate and Tom would take off on their own sometimes leaving Robin and I alone, but that was OK. We just swam, read and sunbathed, and I think he was glad that I was there so that he wasn't a gooseberry when Kate and Tom were around and acting all loved up.

Although I think he still fancied me a bit, he didn't pursue it and I made sure that I didn't give him any signals that I was interested. We kept our chat general – about school and future plans mainly – and I avoided talking about relationship stuff, not that I had that many to talk about, anyway. He had just finished his A-levels and was planning a gap year to travel, so he liked hearing about all the places I'd lived – particularly India, although I was too young to remember a whole lot about being there.

At the end of the second week, Tom's parents went off on a boat trip so the boys took us to see where they were staying. They met us off the bus late morning as usual and then drove us up to the northern tip of the island. I liked it there – it was less built up than the south of the island.

'Wow!' said Kate when Tom stopped the jeep on a slope halfway up a hill and we got out and looked around us.

The views of the coast stretching out down below were awesome – the best I'd seen so far. Tom led the way and we walked down some steps from the parking area towards the house. It felt really private. It was surrounded by olive, pine and fruit trees so that, even if there were neighbours to the left or right, you wouldn't be aware of them. The villa looked like so many on the island with white walls and red-tiled roof but, when we stepped inside, it felt like someone's home, which was nice after the impersonal feel of the bungalows at the centre.

'You going to show us round then?' asked Kate.

Tom immediately went into estate agent mode and gave us a tour. 'Downstairs we 'ave an open-plan sitting room,' he drawled in a rubbish Greek accent, 'At the back is ze kitchen and utility room. At the front, we 'ave a terrace area, then steps down to an infinity pool with the most stunning view of the Aegean in the distance.'

'Crap accent,' said Kate.

'Zank you,' said Tom with a grin.

'Hey, I love these paintings,' I said, noticing some seascapes on the walls in the living room.

'Oh, my gran did those,' said Tom. 'She lived here in her retirement.'

'They're really good,' Kate agreed. 'What's upstairs?'

Tom flashed her a grin, then led us up some stairs, reverting to his terrible accent, which seemed to have changed from bad Greek to a cross between Russian and Welsh.

'Ve 'ave a double bedroom with a balcony at the front,' he said as he showed us around. I noticed that he raised an eyebrow at Kate when he showed us in there and she raised an eyebrow back. 'We 'ave ze twin-bedded rooms, a bath and shower room at the back.'

Kate slapped him playfully. 'Don't ever think of acting,' she said. 'Somehow I don't think it would be the job for you.'

After the tour, we went outside and chilled out around the pool. After a dip, Kate and Tom disappeared inside, leaving Robin and me alone on the sunloungers. He raised an eyebrow and grinned at me. I raised an eyebrow back to let him know that I knew what they were up to.

For a while we read magazines, sunbathed, then swam again and, as I got out of the pool, I noticed Robin watching me. Like *really* watching me with an intense expression on his face. It made me feel uncomfortable and, although I was wearing my turquoise bikini, I felt like I was naked. As soon as I got to my lounger, I pulled my blue sarong out of my bag and draped it round me. Robin continued watching as I reapplied my sun lotion, then looked away as if he was bored, but I felt something in the air that hadn't been there before.

It didn't last long as, minutes later, he disappeared into the villa and came back with a tray loaded down with a carafe of wine, fruit juice, mineral water, pitta bread, hummus, taramasalata, olives and feta cheese.

'Wow. A feast,' I said as he placed the tray on the table by the pool.

'Thought the lady might be hungry,' he replied and made a plate up for me and poured me a glass of wine.

He brought both over and sat on the end of my lounger. I was about to take the plate from him but he shook his head.

'Let me feed you,' he said.

I didn't know what to do. What to say. I didn't want to look like a school kid so tried to appear casual about it. Like I was used to boys feeding me. He put some cheese on the fork, then slowly pushed it into my mouth. I felt myself blush red. I knew he was looking straight into my eyes, but I couldn't meet his gaze and hoped that I didn't look cross-eyed as I tried to focus on the fork. Robin leaned back to the tray, picked up the glass of wine and held it up to my lips.

'Er . . . no . . . thanks. I'll just stick to juice,' I stuttered.

'Try a sip,' he said in a husky voice. 'It's a very good Pinot Grigio. Tom's dad has it flown in especially. You'll like it.'

I felt trapped. I really didn't want to drink wine but I didn't want to appear ungrateful or immature. 'Er . . . I . . .' I began.

Robin took the wine away and took a deep breath. 'Sorry. I keep forgetting. You're younger than Kate, aren't you?'

'I'm fifteen,' I said.

Robin got up, went back to the tray, poured me a glass of juice and handed it to me. 'Here. Juice for the little lady.'

He poured himself a beer and slumped back down on to his lounger. I felt confused and couldn't gauge his mood. Had I upset him? Had he been about to try something then changed his mind? Or had I been imagining it? I thought it was understood that we were just friends.

I drank my juice and felt like I was about nine years old. So uncomfortable. I wished that I could leave and go back to the centre. Anywhere but where I was. I ate half of the lunch that Robin had given me, then lay back, closed my eyes and pretended I was asleep.

Tom and Kate appeared mid-afternoon and for once, Kate looked coy, holding Tom's hand as they came out on to the terrace.

'You two look like you've been up to no good,' said Robin in a strict 'parent' type voice.

For a moment, they both looked sheepish, then Kate said, 'Actually, I was very good, wouldn't you say, Tom?'

Tom laughed and nodded. Robin laughed with him. I attempted to laugh too, but a voice in my head kept telling me that I was fake. Out of my depth. I didn't belong.

Chapter 10

Beach Party

In the early evening, to my relief, we headed back for town where I thought Kate and I would catch the shuttle bus back up to Cloud Nine as we usually did. However, a few moments after we had parked the jeep, a tall girl with long black curly hair came out of one of the local cafés, waved at the boys and made a beeline for us.

'Hey Tom,' she said with a quick appreciative glance in his direction. 'Can you give me a lift to the party?'

Kate took Tom's hand, as if to let her know that they were together, but the girl didn't look bothered. She merely smiled at Kate.

'What party?' Robin asked.

'Out at Troulos beach. Bring your friends,' said the girl. 'It's going to be an all-nighter.'

'OK. Cool. Sure,' said Robin. He looked at Tom and Kate for assent. Both of them nodded enthusiastically. I wasn't even consulted.

The girl was introduced as Andrea and, after Robin and Tom had bought beers and vodka, and Kate, cigarettes, we were back in the jeep headed for the party.

'Don't we need to check it's OK with Aunt Sarah?' I asked. 'She'll be wondering where we are.'

Kate rolled her eyes. 'She probably won't even miss us. And she's got my mobile number, don't forget. Anyway, I reckon we've earned a night off for good behaviour.'

I supposed I must have looked anxious because Kate leaned over and said. 'Don't be a killjoy, India. I mean, it's not exactly like we'll be missing anything except a group hug-in and lentil bake back at the loonie farm. If it makes you happy, I'll give her a call later. I promise. OK?'

'OK.' I made an attempt to smile back at her and as we drove along I tried to talk myself out of the strange mood that had descended on me since Robin had tried to feed me. I felt all wrong. Like I had on the first night up at the centre. Like I was wearing the wrong body.

The word had spread and there were already about fifty party-goers at Troulos beach by the time we got there. More seemed to be arriving by the minute and making their way across the small meadow that led to the beach and ocean. A stage area had been set up on the left-hand side away from the taverna on the right. By the stage was a makeshift bar selling beer and Coke and next to that was a wide barbecue where two sun-grizzled middle-aged men in shorts and red bandannas were cooking fish. A few metres from the sea, someone had built a fire and a bunch of musicians were seated around it – some strumming guitars, others playing congas. A few girls in bikini tops and sarongs were messing about, half dancing to the music and half limbo-ing, while a bunch of teenage boys sat and ogled them.

'It all looks very organised,' I said to Kate as we looked around. 'Look, there are even portaloos over there behind the stage.'

She nodded. 'Yeah. It feels more rock festival than beach party. I guess it's a regular thing out here and why not, hey? They've certainly got the locations.'

We found ourselves a patch of sand a short distance from the stage and Robin got out our supplies. He was about to offer me some vodka but pulled back. 'Oops, forgot. Miss Goodytwoshoes.'

I took the bottle from him. *Maybe it's what I need tonight to loosen up,* I thought, taking a swig. 'Thanks.'

Robin looked pleased. 'Good girl,' he said.

Kate sat snuggled into Tom as the music got going and Robin acted as waiter for the evening, bringing us fish kebabs, peppers and rice from the food stall and keeping us supplied with drinks from our bags. He was so attentive and sweet that I felt bad having given him the brush off earlier. *It must be hard for boys having to make the first move, especially when you have a really good-looking mate like Tom who gets first look in with girls,* I thought, as I watched the sky become a riot of colour – orange, red and purple – turning to translucent turquoise and navy as the sun went down.

'My dad loves sunsets,' I said at one point when Robin and Tom went off to get more beers.

'Me too,' said Kate as she lay back on her elbows.

'This is his favourite time of day. "God's masterpiece work of art," he'd say. Every morning, every evening different.'

'Are you missing him? Them?' Kate asked.

'Nah. Not really,' I replied. For a moment, though, I did feel an ache of homesickness. Dad and I'd watched so many sunsets together all over the world. 'Same old sun wherever you are,' he'd say. I wondered how the sky looked where he was this evening and if he would even get to see any of it or if he was already at work, playing the piano in front of an audience. And I wondered if he ever thought of me.

As the evening went on, everyone seemed in a mellow mood and the feeling of discomfort that I'd had earlier melted away in the glow of the fire and the vodka that Robin kept passing my way.

When the light had gone completely and the sky was velvet black, Tom and Kate took off down the beach as did a number of lovey-dovey couples. Others around the fire seemed to be eyeing each other up, dancing, swaying to the music. I kept an eye out for Joe in the hope that he might be there but there was no sign. There was one cute boy, though, with surfer-blond hair who checked me out at one point when I got up to go to the portaloo, but I didn't hold eye contact with him. I'd had enough of confusing signals for one day.

When Robin went to sit nearer the fire and watch the dancing girls, I got up, walked a short distance down the beach and then went to sit closer to the sea. I was feeling light-headed from the vodka and thought, *I mustn't wander too far – it does look pitch black further along the beach.* I lay down on the cool damp sand and looked up at the sky. I felt all my senses come into sharp focus as I lay there. The smell of the salty air, the aroma of barbecued fish and wood wafting along from the fire, the pungent scent of seaweed, sweat and suntan lotion. As I stared up in the sky, more and more stars began to appear. Like silver dots popping into the black. Pop. Pop. Pop. More and more appeared. Behind me were the sounds of the party, the congas, voices, but where I was felt quieter, with only the gentle lapping of the sea at the water's edge.

I must have drifted off because I awoke with a jerk. I sat up, unsure how long I had been there but I felt cold. I rubbed my arms and was about to get up when I became aware that someone was nearby, coming towards me, but, as the light from the fire was behind them, I could only see a looming shadow. My heart thumped in my chest – I realised that I was probably a little too far away from the party if there was trouble.

'Hey, India, that you?' asked a familiar voice.

'Phew,' I said when I realised that it was Robin. 'You scared me.'

He sat down with a heavy thump on to the sand just behind me. 'Wu*hooooo*,' he said then laughed. 'What you doing out here on your own?'

'Oh nothing – just looking at the sea and the sky.'

Robin snuggled up so that he was right behind me. Then he put his legs around me so that I was seated between his thighs. He pulled me back to lean on his chest. He felt warm and smelled strongly of alcohol and garlic.

'Looking at the sea and the sky and the stars,' he said in a dreamy voice. 'You're a funny girl, aren't you, my little India Jane?'

And then he started kissing the side of my neck and nibbling my ear. I froze. I so didn't want it to be happening.

'No. Robin, I . . .' I tried to move away but it was difficult as he had me firmly between his legs. He manoeuvred himself around to my left, pulled me back further and began to kiss me properly. It was horrible. Too wet. Too full on. As he kissed me and I tried to get away, his breathing grew heavier and he moved his hands up and began to caress my breasts.

I tried to push his hands off. 'Robin, *no*. I don't want . . .'

'Oh come on, India, you know I'm into you,' he groaned. Then he pushed me over so that I was on my back and he was lying on top of me.

'Robin, *NO!*' I cried.

My protest was muffled by the bulk of his body pressing down on me. As I struggled, the sounds all around seemed to grow louder. Behind us, the party blasted on full swing; in front, the waves crashed up on to the beach. The crackle of the fire, the beat of the congas, the strumming guitars, the sound of chatter and laughter. *What am I going to do?* I asked myself as I tried once again to push Robin off and not to panic.

'Where are you?' asked Aunt Sarah in a clipped voice at the other end of the phone. 'Is Kate with you?'

'Yes, she's here. We're at Troulos beach.'

'And Tom and what's his friend's name?'

'Robin. Yes. They're here too.'

'Put Kate on.'

'I . . .'

I didn't know what to do. Kate was slumped by the fire, asleep and had been for over half an hour. 'She's . . . she's asleep.'

'Asleep?' For a moment there was an ominous silence. 'Is she drunk, India Jane?'

I so didn't want to be a snitch, but I couldn't think of how else we'd get home. It was one o'clock in the morning. I was pretty sure that, despite her promise to me, Kate hadn't phoned her mother and I knew that Aunt Sarah would be worried. Both Kate and Tom were well out of it and I knew that no way was he or Robin going to be able to drive us back, especially on roads where there wasn't much lighting. I had no choice but to call Aunt Sarah.

'She's . . . I think she's just tired.'

'Keep your phone switched on and I'll be there as soon as I can.'

'OK. Thanks. I will.'

I made my way back to the fire and sat down to wait. Over by the bar, I could see Robin with his arm around Andrea. They soon started snogging. *At least he wasn't forcing her*, I thought as I glanced away. I felt angry with him. And myself. It was all so stupid and I desperately wanted to get back up to the centre, get under my duvet and forget about the day. Kate was still snoring away at my side, but I was wide awake as I ran through the events of the last few hours in my head for the hundredth time. I'd sobered up fast when Robin had turned into Groper Boy. And I would have been OK if Joe Donahue hadn't come along and tried to do his knight-in-shining armour routine. OK, I was struggling, but I had just been about to try a technique that always worked on Lewis when he had me pinned down during play wrestling fights when we were younger. A swift knee in the groin. It worked every time. However, just as I applied said knee, Robin was suddenly hauled off me and I saw Joe standing there, hands on hips, like a superhero. Ironically, I recalled, he was still wearing his Superman T-shirt. 'Everything all right, India?'

I blustered that I was fine, rolled over and got up swiftly.

Robin also got up, holding his crotch. He hobbled off, muttering something about me being stupid and immature.

'You OK?' Joe asked.

'Fine,' I said again. I felt irritated that he'd caught me being mauled by someone like Robin and so hoped that he hadn't thought that I was in any way complicit. 'He's not my boyfriend or anything.'

'I gathered that,' said Joe. 'In fact I thought you were in trouble.'

'I can handle myself.'

'Yeah? Didn't look like it,' said Joe. 'I'd stay away from those guys if I were you. They're just out to party.'

Before I could stop myself, I blurted. 'Like you care who I hang out with or what I do. And what are you doing down here? Scoring drugs? From what I've heard you like to party yourself.'

Joe looked taken aback at my outburst but he chose to ignore it. 'Look. Why not come over closer to the light area where there are more people. It's dark here.'

'I can look after myself,' I muttered.

'I'm sure you can, but . . .'

'I don't need you looking out for me. I've got three brothers – I don't need another one.' For a moment, at the thought of my brothers, who couldn't even be bothered to send me an e-mail, I felt overwhelmingly alone and that I might cry. I bit my lip instead and pushed the feeling away.

'Whatever,' said Joe. 'Just . . . there are some chancers at these kind of things sometimes. Guys on the look out for . . .' He hesitated for a moment as though searching for words.

'For kids like me? Is that what you were going to say? Go on. Say it. I know you're thinking it. About how pathetic I am. I know that you think I'm a total idiot.'

'I don't actually. I . . . No. I . . . Look, I'm heading back up to the centre. You want a ride?'

I shook my head. 'We have a ride and I have to find Kate. I wouldn't leave without her.'

'Kate can look after herself,' said Joe.

'Maybe but *I* wouldn't leave her,' I said and I knew that I'd said it in a very clipped way as if I was blaming him for something.

Joe looked at me kindly, which made me feel like crying again. 'Good for you, India Jane,' he said. 'It's good to look out for each other.'

I pushed past him and walked towards the fire and it was there that I saw Kate and Tom lying on their backs, snoring away, oblivious to the world. *She clearly hadn't come looking for me*, I thought. I saw Joe check that I was with her then walk off towards the car park.

We should have gone with him, I thought, checking my watch and seeing with horror that it was one in the morning. That's when I called Aunt Sarah. She arrived about twenty-five minutes later and I felt so relieved to see her, even though she was livid. She gave Tom off a real telling-off; then between us, we helped Kate to the car. Kate didn't seemed phased at all. She was well out of her head.

'Mommie dearest,' she slurred. 'Arr. Come to the party. Hurray. Nice to have Mommie dearest here.'

This was a sentiment clearly not shared with Mommie dearest who packed us into the car like naughty five-year-olds and drove us back up the lanes in silence, and I wondered if she was still thinking that Tom Stourton was such a good influence.

Chapter 11

Grounded

I woke at nine-thirty with a cracking headache. It felt as if someone was probing the inside of my brain with ice cold fingers. Horrible. I found a couple of aspirin in Kate's toilet bag and went up to the dining area to get some coffee. I hoped that I might escape Aunt Sarah, but no such luck. She'd been up for hours and was feeling more vocal than last night.

'I would have thought *you'd* have had more sense!' she started when I sat down at her table with my cup of coffee.

She hadn't cooled off over night. Not one bit. She was still mad with me. Still mad with us. Kate was sleeping it off, oblivious to all of it – to what had happened at the party with Robin and to how we got back to the centre.

So I got the full force of the wrath of Aunt Sarah. *Sounds like a movie title,* I thought as she blasted away at me. *The Wrath of Aunt Sarah – a movie coming your way soon.*

She had a list of things to be furious about.

Furious because we were late and had missed supper with her.

Furious because Kate had turned her mobile off.

Furious because neither of us had called.

Furious because 'anything could have happened to us'. (*And almost did*, I thought.)

But most furious because Kate was falling-over drunk and stank of cigarettes. She was so drunk that she'd even offered her mother one before she passed out. I'd never seen Aunt Sarah that mad. It was scary.

And the thing was, I kind of understood. She didn't know where we were. Of course she'd been worried.

'I'm sorry, Aunt Sarah,' I said and I meant it. I felt bad. Bad for her. Bad for Kate. And bad for me.

'I should think that you are, but it's a bit late for apologies, isn't it? What if something had happened to you? Your mother would have killed me. You're in my care while you're here or have you forgotten? I spoke to Fleur and your dad first thing and they'll be calling later. Needless to say, neither of them were very happy to hear about your behaviour and the fact that you'd been drinking too. Don't think you can act the innocent party.'

'That is *so* unfair,' I blurted. 'Why did you have to tell them? For one thing, I didn't even do anything and, for another, I didn't ask to be sent here.'

Aunt Sarah gave me a cool glare and then, suddenly, she looked like a balloon that had been deflated. All the fury went out of her to be replaced with a look of utter weariness.

'You're grounded for the next few days,' she said. 'Both of you. I'm not having either of you going off on your own until you learn to be responsible. You can stay here. At the centre where I can keep an eye on you.'

After the lecture, I grabbed some fruit and escaped up to the cyber office to check my e-mails. There was already one from Mum.

India Jane (not even a dear India Jane, I noted.)
Sarah let us know about last night. What were you thinking of?
Just remember that you're a guest there and . . .

Blah blah blah, like you even care. You're more bothered that Aunt Sarah was upset than by what happened to me, I thought as I scanned the rest of the message to see if Dad had written anything. He hadn't. *Hasn't even got time to be mad with me,* I thought as I pressed delete.

There were two messages from Erin. Just nice, normal mad stuff about spotting Scott Malone outside the chippie on her way home from her supermarket job and there being nothing on telly. (I missed her so much.)

None from the rest of my family. Not even a health warning from Dylan about the dangers of binge drinking.

More and more people were emerging from their bungalows and the centre was starting to buzz with the energy of a new day. As I came down the steps away from reception, I didn't feel like engaging with anyone after my grand telling-off from Aunt Sarah. Not Kate. And especially not Joe. Too late! I rounded a corner and walked smack into him.

'You made it back I see,' he said.

'Yeah. So? Why wouldn't I?' I said, then cursed myself when he looked taken aback by my tone.

'Yes. Why wouldn't you? No. I mean . . . I know, just . . . oh never mind,' he blustered.

Say something funny, said a voice in my head. *Say something funny.* What came out was: 'Yes and I've just had breakfast. Surprisingly I can feed myself too.'

Nooooooooooooooo. Idiot, said the voice in my head. *Now, zip it, India. Be quiet. Shut up. Shut up. Oh God,* I thought, seeing a wall go up in Joe's eyes. *He thinks I am a stroppy cow. He's right. I am. But I'm so not. Not really. No. The real me is still in here somewhere, I wanted to say. You'd like her. She's nice.* But, of course, nothing came out.

The conversation had gone all wrong. I had no idea why I was so hostile to him, especially when he had only tried to help last night and he wasn't the one who had tried to maul me. *I must be nicer,* I thought, and tried to think of something friendly to say.

'Er . . . I noticed you had a Superman T-shirt on yesterday,' I started.

117

He nodded.

'Isn't he the one who wears his underpants over his trousers? Maybe you should do that. You know, complete the look.'

Noooooooooooooooooooooooooooooooooo. What in God's name made me say that? I thought as the words came out of my mouth.

Joe burst out laughing and shook his head. 'Yeah. Yeah, he is. I'll keep that in mind next time I wear that T-shirt. I'll wear my boxers on the outside just for you. I'll see if it helps me get lucky.' And he went off towards the dining area chuckling to himself.

'Arghhhhh,' I muttered, and kicked the wall of the reception bungalow just as Anisha was going up the steps.

She glanced after Joe. 'Boy trouble?' she asked.

'No. *No.* Why would it be?'

She held her hands up. 'Woah. Just asking. I thought I saw you chatting to Joe. Forget I asked.'

'No. I wasn't . . . At least, I was. Chatting. He's . . . I don't even know him, at least, I do, but not really.'

Anisha laughed. 'You sound confused,' she said.

'I am. I . . . Oh, I don't know. I always seem to say or do the wrong thing when he's around. And . . . I just don't get him.'

Anisha looked thoughtful and nodded. 'Yeah. I guess he is a bit of a mystery. Me and my mate Rosie were talking about him last night. Neither of us can work him out either.'

'He seems to like being on his own.'

'Yeah,' she said, smiling. 'Cute though, hey?'

I nodded and Anisha went up to take her place behind reception. I felt bad. Whoever Joe was, mystery man or superhero, I'd been rude to him and then said something stupid. Again. When I wasn't acting like the village idiot in front of him, I was acting the strop queen. Suddenly I desperately wanted to get away on my own. Clear my head of the whirlpool of thoughts spinning around.

'Where's quiet near here?' I asked Anisha.

'Like no people quiet?'

I nodded.

Anisha thought for a moment. 'At this time of day, the beach at the bottom of the slope down through the trees on the left. Totally private. Lovely. I always take off down there when I want space. It's quiet in the morning, then it fills up early afternoon.'

Perfect – and Aunt Sarah can't object because the beach is still part of the complex, I thought. I thanked Anisha and set off in the direction she'd pointed in.

I passed through the bungalow area where already some of the morning classes had started. *Not for me,* I thought, watching a bunch of middle-aged ladies swaying to some sort of weird pipe music. I left the accommodation area, headed down the slope, across a meadow then over towards the sea. The ground felt baked dry as I made my way down the path, through the welcome shade of an area with pine trees and then out on to the beach. Anisha was right: it was a lovely sheltered cove and was empty. With a sigh of relief, I walked about halfway down, then plonked myself on to the sand and stared out at the waves.

It was only eleven, but it was hot hot hot and airless, and I cursed the fact that I hadn't thought to bring a magazine or book down with me. Or suntan lotion. Mum would go mad if she knew I was sitting here without my factor twenty.

Two weeks down, two more to go, I thought, watching the waves lap up and make lace patterns as they broke on to the shore. *And how different everywhere looks to last night.* Everywhere was bleached bright with the sun this morning, all shadows blasted away. It felt safe. Last night on the beach had felt dark and dangerous.

I reached into my bag for my mobile. Even though it cost a fortune to call Erin, I didn't care – I needed to hear her voice. I was about to try her number, but then I remembered that Greece is two hours ahead. It would only be nine in Ireland. She would kill me if I woke her up on her day off – and I had enough people mad at me for the time being.

Now what? I asked myself. *What am I going to do?* I felt restless and out of sorts. In front was the ocean. To my left and right, the beach, behind me, trees. *Where do I fit? Not up at the centre with the swaying loonies, nor with the crowd who were down on the beach last night. I am the odd girl out. I don't belong with Kate and the boys. I'm not a party girl like her or them. I was kidding myself. Trying to talk myself into being someone I'm not. All the time, I was out of place. I felt fake. But I don't fit up at Cloud Nine either. No way. All of the guests were there voluntarily. They'd paid to come. Not forced to, like me, because I was in the way of my parents' plans.* When I thought of Mum and Dad and Dylan and Lewis, tears came to my eyes. I felt such an ache deep inside – the most homesick I had felt since I had arrived. Even though the Notting Hill house was the beginning of a new chapter, I couldn't wait to get back there and start it. *All I want is a home,* I thought. *A place where I belong, with a mum and dad who are interested in what I'm up to and what I'm thinking about. I want a family who cares. A bunch of mates I really get on with. I want a room of my own. Somewhere I can be myself and be happy.*

As the sun rose in the sky, the temperature became more and more furnace-like, so that even the sand grew hot to touch. It was so hot that you could see the heat shimmering in the air. I still felt restless, and there was only so long that I could stare at the sea and think deep thoughts about my place in the universe. *I have to go back up to the centre,* I thought. *Get my baseball cap, my sun lotion and something to do.*

As I walked back over the beach, I noticed that a group of people from the centre had come down and were sitting by the path in a clearing in the shade of the trees. There were about twelve of them, all dressed in white, seated in a semicircle around a slim Indian man, whom I vaguely recognised from posters that I'd seen around the centre. He looked about forty and was sitting cross-legged in front of them. I had no choice but to walk by and was trying to do so without disturbing them when he saw me creeping past and gave me a huge beam.

121

'Ah, a latecomer! Come, sit. Be comfortable,' he said.

He was smiling at me with such warmth that I felt it would be rude not to accept his invitation. I tiptoed over to the side of the group and sat down. Liam, the boy who had been friendly to me on the first day, was next to me and nodded.

Someone had lit a sandalwood joss stick which wafted across the area. The scent reminded me of home and Mum's experiments with her oils, and it felt pleasant to be in the shade of the trees after the heat of the sun. I wasn't really in a hurry to go back up to the bungalow and Kate. She was bound to be in a strop when she heard that we were grounded. I didn't want to do any of the other classes so I began to listen to the man.

'The problem isn't the bomb,' he said. 'The problem is the minds that created the bomb. Wars will never be stopped by more wars. Peace will only come about when the *minds* of men are at peace. If a mind is at peace then what need is there to create destruction or bombs? For example, take a knife. It is a tool which you can use to cut an apple or to stab a man. It is the intention of the user of the tool that determines if something is destructive or not, not the thing itself. So what mankind needs is peace of mind. What we all need is peace of mind.'

Yeah, that's true, I guess, I thought, looking around at the group. They were a mixed bunch in race and age. Some, like Liam, looked not much older than me, others were in their twenties or thirties, and others looked like they were well into their sixties if not older. They all had one thing in common though. As they sat listening, they appeared so still, many with smiles of contentment on their faces as they gazed at the speaker in front of them. I turned my attention back to him. He spoke with a slight Indian accent and his voice was soft and low, easy to listen to. But there was something else about him. He glowed as if he'd been polished inside and out, as if he'd been on the best detox diet ever invented. He radiated good health and well-being. At first I'd put him at about forty, but his smooth face was ageless and unlined and, like his followers, he gave out an aura of tranquillity.

'The peace you seek is within you,' he continued, 'each and everyone of you. You will never find it outside in the material things that claim to give you happiness. Nor is your true home on the planet, although we fool ourselves that we belong in a place or a country. No. Tell me, my friends, have any of you ever felt that you don't fit in this world? You don't belong?'

To my amazement, all of the group put up their hands. And so did I.

The speaker smiled. 'That is because your true home is not in this world. Your true home is deep within you, in a place of peace that you can reach through meditation. It is there that you will find true contentment. Everything in this life is always changing. That is its nature. Pain comes about because people want things to stay the same, but that cannot be and we have no control to prevent it. Like a river, our lives roll on. Our present becomes the past and time flows on to a largely unknown future. The only thing that never changes is the life force that is behind everything. That life force is inside each of you. As long as you have breath, that life force is within you and when you find that, you will find peace and become a human being as opposed to a human doing.'

As I listened, a feeling of calm came over me and the restlessness that I'd felt earlier faded away. It was like he was speaking my experience. Everything I'd been thinking out on the beach. Maybe I wasn't alone, the odd one out after all. It seemed that all these people sitting here with me felt the same way.

As I continued listening, I remembered the time when Erin and I had attempted to learn to meditate. We'd got a book out of the school library on the subject and taken it back to her place to try out. First it said to sit in the lotus position – the position I noted the teacher was sitting in. It's not easy. You cross your legs but put your feet up on your thighs so that the sole of the foot faces upwards. I could do it easily but Erin groaned in agony. Her feet just wouldn't go where she wanted them to.

'Easy for me,' I'd said to her, 'because I'm a superior soul on my thousandth incarnation whereas you are a low life. Probably your first time on the planet in fact.'

She'd bashed me over the head with a pillow in response.

The book said that we had to concentrate our minds by saying a mantra, *Om Shanti*, over and over again. At first we had to say it out loud and then internalise it. We dutifully did as instructed and, when I opened my eyes, fifteen minutes later,

Erin was flat out on the floor, sleeping like a baby. 'We don't even know what *Om Shanti* means,' she said in her defence. 'It might mean dog's bollocks in Swahili so we've been sitting here saying dog's bollocks over and over.'

Somehow I didn't think either of us had the right attitude and we discovered boys soon after, so never really gave it a proper chance. *Maybe now's the time,* I thought, as the lecture wrapped up and I got up with the others to make my way back up to the centre. I did feel better, like some of the speaker's serenity had rubbed off on me. Maybe there was more to meditation than snoring on the floor. Everything the speaker had said made such good sense. He'd given me food for thought. Maybe I'd attend some more of the talks. Maybe I'd even learn how to meditate properly.

I certainly had nothing else to do.

Chapter 12

This Way to Paradise

'Give me a break, India Jane,' said Kate as she sat up in bed and rubbed her eyes. 'What time is it?'

'Half ten.'

Kate snuggled back down in bed again. 'Way too early,' she said. 'I suppose you've been up since dawn communicating with God and giving flowers to policemen.'

'No.'

'So where have you been? And why are you all dressed in white?'

'No reason.' I didn't tell her that this afternoon, I was going to attend my first proper meditation session. We'd been asked to wear white to symbolise purity. She'd only make fun.

'So where have you been?'

'I went to sit in on the early meditation session with the others.'

'I thought you hadn't learnt how to do it yet.'

'I haven't, but I like to go and sit when the others do it. There's a really peaceful vibe there.'

'Jesus, India Jane, I'm beginning to worry about your sanity. I mean, hanging with that bunch of nutters? Talking about vibes? Please don't tell me that you're serious.'

'Just checking it out. Don't worry,' I replied. 'I have to do *something* while we're here. And even though you sneak out every night, we *are* still meant to be grounded.'

Kate raised an eyebrow. 'Goodytwoshoes,' she said. 'And Mum only said we were grounded for a few days. I think she's chilled out a bit now, especially since my exam results came through and I did better than she'd thought. She's re-owned me again. So you could always come with me. I don't think Mum would mind if you stayed out a bit late.'

'No way. I don't want to see Robin again — '

'He feels bad about what happened, you know,' Kate interrupted. 'He told Tom. I think it was the booze and, you know Robin, he's not a bad guy underneath — '

'I don't care. I still don't want to see him. I don't think we could go back to being friends.'

Kate shrugged. 'Maybe not, but cut him some slack, like, he said you were putting out signals — '

'I *so* was not! How could he even say that? And how could

you believe him? You knew I didn't fancy him.'

For a moment there was an uncomfortable silence in the room and we both turned away from each other. I felt mad with Kate for taking Robin's side.

'And, anyway, you shouldn't be seeing those guys,' I said. 'I bet your mum wouldn't like it, if she knew you still were.'

'Well, actually, for your information, Tom wrote a note to Mum apologising and saying it wouldn't happen again, so there.'

'Really?'

Kate nodded. 'Yeah and you know how desperate Mum is to get in with his mum and dad. Mum said I could see him as long as I don't stay out too late. I would have filled you in, if you hadn't had your head stuck in the clouds for the last few days.'

This struck me as quite funny. 'Well, we are on Cloud Nine,' I said.

Kate didn't laugh. 'I've got to hang out with someone and you're not exactly available any more. Come out with us.'

'I don't want to. I don't want to see Robin. I've got nothing to say to him. And, anyway, your mum might have chilled out, but my mum's still cross with me and, don't forget, it was me who got the full force from Aunt Sarah after that night on the beach. She'd calmed down a bit when you finally crawled out of bed.'

'Like you're going to let me forget! Oh, don't let's be cross with each other, Indie J, please. And, believe it or not, I am concerned about you – that you're having a good holiday here.

I mean, I appreciate that, yes, we do have to do something to kill the time, but why not paint or learn to dance? Get in touch with your inner wombat or something. Anything but join the holier than thou brigade.'

'I won't. I haven't. And they're not holier than thou. They talk a lot of sense. As I said, I'm just checking it all out.'

It was four days since I'd first seen the meditation instructor down on the beach. His name was Sensei – which means teacher – and he'd flown in the night before the first meeting down on the beach. I'd seen the posters advertising his arrival around the centre but hadn't taken much notice of them because I wasn't interested at the time. Now that I was, Liam told me all about him. Since that first encounter, I'd been every day to listen to him talk and, the more I'd heard, the more I liked what he had to say. He was about the same age as my father, but about as opposite to my dad as you could ever meet. He radiated serenity whereas Dad exuded chaos. I'd sneaked a peak into Sensei's room one day – Liam had shown me, and it was amazing. Even his room had an aura of peace. A few simple things. The lingering scent of sandalwood joss stick. Dad was like Kate, leaving a trail of stuff wherever he went as a clear demonstration that he had passed through.

'OK, so you're checking it out. What have you discovered then?' Kate insisted.

'Oh . . . it's hard to describe . . .' I started, though I wished I'd kept my mouth shut about it to her. While it made sense when

I was with Liam or listening to Sensei, I couldn't articulate what I felt to her. All I knew was that I'd found something I wanted to learn how to do. And people I wanted to be like. Through meditation, I was going to become the new me. Serene me. At peace with the world.

Erin was also dubious about my 'initiation' when I got through to her during her break on my mobile an hour later. It was almost time for the session and I was feeling excited but also a tad anxious, which is why I wanted to speak to her rather than text. Liam kept telling me that the first proper meditation could be like a rebirth for some people; for others it was like having their third eye opened. What was going to happen? Would I see a vision or something? I didn't know, but I had to share what I was feeling with someone.

'Will you have to wear a sari?' Erin asked after I'd filled her in on the latest.

'No. At least I don't think so.' I didn't tell her that I was dressed in white.

'Are there any fit boys in the group?'

'Boys? Er . . . not really. No one I fancy, anyhow. It's *so* not about that.'

'Go back to the er, not really. I know you, India Jane. There's something you're not telling me. Who is the er, not really?'

I laughed. I could never hide anything from Erin. Not even when we were in different countries. 'Oh, you know. He's not really my type, but OK, yes, there is a guy in the group, Liam, who is halfway decent. I don't fancy him, although he's OK-looking . . . but he's growing on me.'

'Growing? Hmm. He sounds like a kind of fungus. Details,' Erin demanded. 'Describe.'

'Tall. He's seventeen. Thin. Not conventionally good-looking but he's got an interesting face. He's got something about him. Charisma. I could imagine him being some kind of leader or director when he's older. Er . . . what else? He's got a long nose, um, interesting eyes . . .'

'Interesting eyes? What? Like he's got three of them? Is that because of that third eye thing you were on about yesterday?'

'No, dozo. He has two. They're brown, smallish but sharp, like a bird's eyes, taking everything in, you know? And when he looks at me, it's like he really looks. Like he's looking right into me.'

'Yuk. Like into your lungs, your liver and kidneys?'

'*Eriiiin.*'

'Sorry, just messing. How do you feel when he looks at you?'

'Normal. Why?'

'The eye magnet thing. Do you get the eye magnet thing?'

'What's the eye magnet thing?' Erin was always coming up with strange terms for checking if attraction to a boy was real or not. This was a new one on me.

'It's when a boy looks at you and you lock eyes for a moment more than is normally necessary – as if your eyes are magnets and you can't tear yourself away from looking at each other. It's usually accompanied by a stomach lurch.'

'Sounds like some kind of nasty physical disease.'

'It is,' said Erin. 'It's called love. So. Liam's lips?'

'Yes. He has lips.'

'*India*. Describe them. I have to have a picture. You know that.'

'OK. Just lips. I haven't really noticed.'

'Hah! Then he can't be growing on you in a fancying kind of way. If he was, you'd be able to describe his mouth exactly. Shoes?'

I laughed. Erin always said you can tell a lot about a boy by his shoes. 'Sandals.'

'Bin him. Don't get involved. We don't do boys in sandals, India. You know that.'

'Forget what he looks like, Erin, or what he wears. I don't care about that. It's like he gets me, you know? I can really talk to him and he understands what I'm going through and he was the only person who was friendly when I arrived.'

'Does he have a girlfriend?'

'Don't think he's bothered about relationships, although he does hang out with a girl called Rosie. She's in the group and is nice too.'

'Hhm. Is he gay?'

'Don't think so.'

'And he's halfway decent you say? Not sure I like the sound

of him, India. For one thing, I thought we didn't do halfway. We don't do sandals and we don't do compromise. Remember? We are going to hold out for princes and suffer no frogs along the way. Talking of princes, what about Prince Cutenick himself? Joe?'

'Disaster. He spends all his time either in the art room or at the bar he works at down in town or off on mystery trips. I'm keeping out of his way for the rest of the holiday.'

'Oh really? Why?'

'He's . . . I don't know. He seems to bring out the worst in me. I act like a twit when he's around and talk rubbish.'

'Ah. Sounds like love to me. Let me know if the eye magnet thing happens with him.'

'It won't. I'm totally off boys for the rest of the holiday. It's weird because, since I met Sensei and Liam, I am totally cool about Joe. Really. Like what he thinks of me doesn't matter any more. All I want is to learn this meditation and find peace of mind. Liam says he thinks that it may be what's been missing from my life so far.'

'So far? What does he know? India, we're only fifteen. There are loads of things we have to try still, loads of things that are missing.'

'I know but . . . oh, I can't explain, Erin. Sometimes when I'm listening to Sensei, I feel so . . . oh, I can't put it into words, like I've been waiting all my life to get here and hear his message.'

'Woah, India . . .'

'I've been waiting all week to learn how to meditate and this afternoon I'm going to learn.'

'*Om Shanti* and och aye the noo. Remember when we tried meditation?'

'Yeah. But we didn't do it properly,' I said. 'I've been listening about it for days now and you have to put some commitment in.'

'Listening? Sure they're not brainwashing you?'

'No. Course not. This guy, he's, like, so inspiring.'

'Who is he exactly again?'

'Sensei. He's from India. He's about forty. He's been teaching meditation for years. He travels the world doing it.'

'So is he Hindu or Buddhist?'

'He's not any religion, although Liam says that the word *sensei* is Buddhist and he teaches a Buddhist meditation. But he's not about getting people to join a religion or take on any lifestyle. He simply wants to show people a way to find inner peace.'

Erin was quiet for a while. 'Hey, India Jane,' she said finally. 'Be careful, hey. I've heard of people getting involved in cults and stuff.'

'No way, Erin. This isn't a cult. And I'm not stupid.'

'Maybe not, but you sound . . . well, you sound kind of intense. Not like you.'

'Nah. You're imagining it. It's me. Still me. Mad. Mixed up.'

'Good. That's OK, then. Keep me informed, OK? Don't sell your soul . . .'

'Not unless they offer a good price.'

'In that case, they can have mine too.' Erin laughed. 'That's more like it. Don't lose your sense of humour. And don't give up on this Joe guy. I like the look of him from that pic you sent. And he has a nice mouth.'

'I am so totally over him, Erin. Really.'

'If you say so. As I said, keep me updated and, if you snog him, I want details. And report back to me after the ceremony or session or whatever. I need to know that you haven't decided to join a nunnery.'

'I will. But enough about me. What about you?'

'What about me?'

'How are you?'

'Ah. At last! I thought you'd *never* ask. And since you are asking, it's a fine day here in Dublin and last night I was captured by Martians who ate my brain.'

'So no change there, then.'

'No, but thanks for asking. Nice to feel you're taking an interest.'

'Nah. Just faking it to be polite.'

'No change there, then.'

'Nah,' I said. 'Seriously though, I was a bit worried that I'd been a bit me me me lately.'

'Nah. OK, a bit. But you don't do it all the time, so it's OK.

Besides, what are friends for, if not to listen through sickness and through health, through richer and through poorer?'

'That's marriage. The Martians have eaten your brain.'

'Told you. No. I'm fine, honest. Not a lot happening here.'

I love Erin.

We couldn't talk much longer as she was on a break and had to go but, once again, I so wished she was with me. What was happening to me felt major and I liked to share all the big things in my life with her.

The sense of anticipation I'd been feeling grew as I made my way into the place that had been allotted as the meditation room. Like all the bungalows used for the different classes at the centre, it was a simple white room with parquet flooring. Liam and Rosie were already there when I arrived and were lighting the usual sandalwood joss stick, opening windows to let a breeze blow through and placing mats and cushions out on the floor.

'Sit down,' said Liam, indicating a cushion. 'The others are on their way. How are you feeling?'

I pulled a face as if to say, not sure.

'Big day for you huh?' he asked.

I nodded.

'When the student is ready, the Master appears,' said Liam. 'It's no accident that you're here on this island at this time. It is your destiny.'

Wow, I thought. *Big words.* But there was a part of me that felt that it was fated. Meant to be. Destiny had brought me here to find peace of mind.

Rosie gave me her wide smile. 'You're so lucky,' she said. 'Some souls have to wait lifetimes to meet their Master.'

I could hear Erin's voice in my head. *Like, woah. I've only come to learn some meditation techniques, not meet my Master.*

The other people for the session began to arrive and, like me, they were dressed in white. There was Marjorie Stott, a gentle old lady from Bristol. I liked her. We'd had a chat at breakfast one morning. Her husband had died two years previously and coming to Cloud Nine was her first real trip without him. She was missing him terribly. Brian McClary was another. He was a student from Dingle Bay in Ireland. The trip to Cloud Nine was part of his gap year. I wasn't so keen on him. He wore socks with his sandals, had lily-white hairy legs and wore shorts that were *way* too short. Like, had he never heard of Bermudas? I tried to tell myself not to be shallow, that looks weren't everything and that I should look for the person within, but even so, his long pimply legs were not a pretty sight. And lastly there was Clare Taylor. She had just finished her first year as an infant school teacher and said she needed to find peace of mind to help her cope with the kids. She had wild 'I've stuck my finger in the electric socket' brown hair, a round jolly face and was always smiling.

Sensei arrived soon after the others and sat on his cushion at the front. Liam and Rosie took places at the back near the door and a mad thought went through my head. *They're blocking the exits. Run for it now.* I told myself not to be stupid. Aunt Sarah would never let anyone who wasn't legit teach at her centre.

Sensei closed his eyes and for a few moments sat in silence and, once again, it struck me how still and serene he was. He was beautiful to watch but, as the minutes ticked on, I wondered, *Is this it? Should I be doing the same?*

Sensei opened his eyes and beamed at all of us. 'So let us begin. First, I am going to talk to you about the sea. You have all seen the sea, yes? When we look at the ocean, we see the waves on the surface – sometimes they're calm, sometimes choppy and yet, if you go deep into the ocean, deep, deep, fathom deep, regardless of what is happening on the surface, there is stillness, there is tranquillity. In the same way, your mind is like the sea.'

OK, my mind is like the sea, I thought and then a voice suddenly started singing in my head. *Oh, I do like to be beside the seaside . . .*

Shut up, said a second voice.

You shut up too, said a third voice.

Listen to Sensei, said a fourth. I made myself concentrate.

'On the surface of the mind, there are thoughts and feelings and, like the waves on the sea, these thoughts are sometimes calm, sometimes choppy. Yes?'

We all nodded.

'In order to find peace, you must go deep inside of yourself beneath the waves of emotion. This is why we are here this afternoon – to find this stillness. Turning inside: this is the way to paradise, the state of being that so many seek externally. It is within you, not outside.'

That's what I want to do, I thought. *Find stillness. Get away from all the contradictory feelings inside me and these nutty voices in my head on the surface of my sea or mind or whatever. Find this way to paradise.*

Sensei nodded at Liam, who got up and closed the shutters at the window and the room grew dark. *Wuhoohooo,* said one of the nutters in a scary voice in my head.

'This method I am going to teach you is a Vipassana meditation derived from the school of Theravadin Buddhism and is believed by many to be the original method that the Buddha himself taught . . .'

Cool, I thought.

Theravadin, isn't that a kind of turtle? asked another voice.

Nope, that's a terrapin. Now shut up and CONcentrate, said a third.

'We will start by concentrating on the breath. This will bring you into the present moment . . .' Sensei continued.

Suddenly I was aware of a new voice in my head singing in a broad Scottish accent. *Let the wind blow high and the wind blow low, through the streets in my kilt I go. All the lassies cry, Hello! Donald, where's your trousers?*

Oh my God! I thought. *Where did that come from? Oh, I remember.* It was a song that Erin's mum used to sing sometimes when she was cooking. It used to make us laugh because she is Irish and yet she liked to sing Scottish songs. *I am going mad. Shut up mind. Shut up, shut up, shut up.* I made an effort to refocus on what Sensei was saying.

'Although your thoughts may be preoccupied with the past or the future, the breath is always in the present. If it wasn't, we wouldn't be alive. However, few people live in the here and now because thoughts, goals, dreams or memories occupy so much of our attention, making us think about past occurrences or future deadlines, appointments and plans.'

Boooooooring, said a very loud voice in my mind just as Sensei looked my way. *Oh God. What if he can read people's minds? I bet he can, being a holy man. And I'm not really bored. I'm interested. I am.* I blushed deep red and looked at the floor.

'How often do we wish away the week, wishing it was the weekend? Or spend a day at work or school, wishing it was home time?' Sensei continued. 'Always wanting to be where we're not. So often happiness seems to lie at any time apart from the present moment . . .'

That's actually true, I thought. *Like me on the island. I've wanted to be anywhere else but here since I arrived, always thinking I'll only be happy when I'm back home in London or with Erin. Yeah. It's true.*

'It is only in the present that true happiness lies and this meditation is a technique to bring your awareness into the moment so that you can experience its perfection. OK. Are you all sitting comfortably? Relaxed?'

Everyone shifted about a little. Mrs Stott coughed. Brian sniffed loudly, then the room grew quiet again.

'OK, close your eyes,' said Sensei. 'I'm going to teach you two methods of focus. Both are equally effective. Try them both and later you can choose which works best for you. First, focus your attention on the breath as it enters the tip of your nostrils . . .'

'Er, Sensei, I have a blocked nose,' Brian interrupted.

'No problem,' said Sensei. 'Simply focus on the breath going into your mouth. OK. Now feel the cold air being breathed in. Yes. Then warm air being breathed out a moment later. Yes. Good. Don't attempt to follow the breath down to the lungs but keep your attention fixed on the nostrils. Imagine that you are a sentry at a gate watching and noting who in entering and who is leaving as you breathe in and out.'

Yeah. I can do this, I thought, focusing my attention as Sensei had directed. The room grew quiet as each of us concentrated on our breath. It felt nice for a while and then the loonie brigade that lives in my head started up again.

Open your eyes – see what everyone else is doing.

No. No. Sensei might be watching.

Yeah. Give this a proper try. Stop messing about. Concentrate like Sensei said.

He is the Master. Master Bates, tee hee hee hee. Oh God, that's an old joke of Ethan's.

Nickynockynoodles.

Whadt? I am mad. There's no hope. No. No. I'm not mad. These thoughts are just the surface of the ocean and it's choppy. Go deeper. Find the peace. Focus. Focus.

Cold breath in. Warm breath out. Or was it the other way round? Warm breath in. Cold breath out. No. Can't be that way round, stupid. OK. Start again.

I am a fish swimming in the sea of my mind.

I wonder what Joe's doing. Erin said to report back to her if there is any snogging activity. I wish. No, I don't. Scrap that thought. I don't care about him. I hate him. I wonder what he'd be like to kiss. Erin's right. He has got a nice mouth. I bet he's a really good kisser.

I felt a lovely feeling in my stomach when for a moment I imagined kissing Joe.

Focus, idiot. You're supposed to be concentrating, not thinking about kissing some boy who's not even interested.

So why isn't he interested? What's wrong with me? Maybe I should confront him. No. Bad idea. Boys hate that.

Sensei's voice suddenly brought me back into the room. 'And now, the second method,' he said as I realised I had hardly given the first method half a chance. 'This time, focus your attention on the rise and the fall of the abdomen as you inhale and exhale. Simply concentrate on the motion of the abdomen as you breathe.'

I followed his instructions and it was true, my abdomen did go up and down as I breathed in and out and, for a few minutes, I managed to stay focused.

And then: *I'll go up to the dining area and get a juice after this. I'm thirsty.*

And I want a wee.

And my left leg is itchy.

My right leg's gone to sleep.

Actually I could do with a sleep. I was up so early this morning. I could curl up on the floor and doze off right now.

Jesus, this is boring. How long have we been doing it?

I wonder what Dad would make of me meditating? Does he even care what I get up to these days? I wonder why it all changed with him. There was a time when he knew everything I did. Was interested. Sad really.

I feel alone in the world lately. Unloved. Like no one really cares.

India. Stop feeling sorry for yourself and concentrate.

Oh yeah.

Up . . . down. Cold air in. Warm out. Abdomen up, abdomen down. Boring boring. My bum hurts on this hard floor.

This isn't paradise. Not outside. Not inside.

I opened my eyes and took at peek at the others.

The room was still in darkness, silent. *How much longer to go?* I wondered as I strained to see my watch in the dim light.

Let me out of here, chorused all the voices.

'Whichever method you choose,' said Sensei, 'watch your breath with total awareness. As the sensation of stillness grows, be aware of how your body feels . . .'

Yeah, yeah, whatever. Wind it up, holy guy, said the renegade that lives in my head. Sensei continued talking but I couldn't really take it in. My mind was all over the place. *Heck. I am sooooooo crap at this*, I thought. *I am clearly not cut out for meditation. Not one bit. Not a chance. No way.*

Chapter 13

Persuasion

I raced back up to my room after the session. I wanted to talk to someone I knew and was hoping that Kate would be there, but our little bungalow was empty. I felt strange after the session, like premenstrual times ten, which was weird because it wasn't that time of the month. Marjorie, Brian and Clare had looked blissed out as we filed out of the bungalow and were gushing about what a wonderful experience they'd had. Liam and Rosie too. For me it had been a total anticlimax and, once again, I felt like the odd girl out. I seemed to be the only one who hadn't got much out of it and seeing their enthusiasm made me feel like a failure. I had an overwhelming desire to speak to Mum or even Dad. To be told that I was OK. It didn't matter that I couldn't meditate or that I had a coachload of mad people living in my head. That I was still loved.

I tried both their numbers, but both mobiles were on voicemail. Hearing Dad's voice brought tears to my eyes. *Woah, I really am feeling emotional,* I thought as I brushed them aside.

Next I tried Erin. Her phone was on voicemail too.

I tried Ethan. *Great,* I thought as he picked up and I heard his familiar voice. I sat back on my bed, ready to have a good heart to heart. Ethan was always so good at listening and saying the right thing. 'Hey, India,' he said. 'How . . . NOOOOOOOO. Lara! Put that down. Oh God, India. Sorry. I'm in charge of the twins here. No! Lara! So sorry, India. Bad timing. Got to go, Lara's just plastered nail polish all over the wall. Speak later?'

'Sure,' I said. 'Is . . . is Jessica there?' My sister-in-law was a good listener too.

But Ethan didn't reply. He'd already hung up.

Next I tried Lewis. His flatmate, Chaz, picked up. 'Nah. Dunno where he is,' he said.

'Will you ask him to call his sister, India.'

'Call his sister in India?'

'No, his *sister* India. That's me. India Jane. In Greece.'

'Oh right,' said Chaz, laughing. 'Complicated. OK. Call sister.'

I knew he wouldn't. For one thing, Chaz didn't ask for my number and, knowing how disorganised Lewis was, he wouldn't have it anywhere.

And so to the strange little medically obsessed squirt, I thought as I tried Dylan's mobile. Even the idea of speaking to him was appealing. *We could have a conversation about melanomas or irritable bowel syndrome,* I thought as his phone rang. *Anything to remind me that I have a home life somewhere. That I do actually belong some place.*

His voicemail was on. *That's it then,* I thought. *My whole family unavailable. All have busy lives. Lives that don't involve me. And I don't think my dad even likes me any more.*

I felt lonely and sorry for myself and was just getting ready for a good blub when my phone rang. It was Erin and she listened patiently while I poured out the events and feelings of the morning. *Thank God for mates,* I thought as she laughed her head off when I told her about my rubbish attempts to meditate.

'I am so relieved, India,' she said. 'I seriously thought you were going to join the God squad.'

'I tried. Maybe some other time, when I'm older. It's like there are four radio stations playing in my head all at the same time.'

'Well, you are a Gemini, sign of the twins, split personality and all that.'

'Yeah, but there are more than a couple of personalities in my head. There's like a whole coachload. I felt like such a failure.'

'Rubbish. It's just not your thing. Give yourself a break. So what now? You still have about a week and a half there. Are you going to give in to your desires and pursue the lowly path of boys, clothes and chocolate?'

'Sounds good to me,' I said. 'Lead the way.'

'Right. Let's make a plan for you to seduce Joe.'

'Joe? No. I *told* you. He's soooo not interested, although I did see him watching when we came out of the meditation session. Like he was surprised to see me in there with those guys. No doubt he thinks it's all rubbish. He's just the type to make fun of something like that.'

'Go and ask what he's doing tonight. And don't mention the meditation if you think that he's not interested.'

'Can't tonight. Liam said he's going to do a picnic hamper for us to take down on to the beach here. To celebrate my first meditation session.'

'First and last by the sound of it.'

'He'll understand that it's not my thing. They're not into pressurising people. That was made clear from the beginning.'

'So just chill out,' said Erin. 'Enjoy being where you are. Find the middle way and all that Zen stuff.'

'You are very wise Obi-Wan Kenobi.'

'I know. I am actually the chosen one, but don't let on to many people or I'll be mobbed whilst I'm stacking the shelves with tins of podded peas and that really won't be good timing. My boss makes all her workers wear these most unattractive hairnets and I want to be looking my best when I come out as the incarnation of goddessdom.'

Poor Erin, I thought after I'd put the phone down. *There she is slaving away in her holiday job, and she never seriously complains*

although it can't be much fun. And here's me, on an idyllic island in the
sun and grouching about like Queen Grouch herself. From now on, I'm
going to make the most of being here and stop being so self-obsessed.
Talking to her had made me feel so much better. She made
everything sound so simple – that, even though the meditation
wasn't for me, it wasn't any big deal. Somehow I'd managed to
blow it all out of proportion. It didn't mean I was the saddo
failure that I had thought I was.

A few hours later, I was sitting down on the beach with Liam.
It was a lovely warm evening with a gentle breeze and we'd just
eaten the most scrummy supper of red peppers, zucchini, herbs,
cheese and gorgeous olives followed by tiny Greek sweets made
with syrup and pistachios and one divine cake made with
cinnamon.

'My dad calls me Cinnamon Girl,' I said, licking honey and
spices off my fingers.

He reached over and pushed a loose strand of hair behind my
ear. 'Because of your beautiful hair,' he said, and looked deeply
into my eyes in a way that made me feel really uncomfortable.
'It looks like burnished copper when the sun catches it.'

'Er . . . yeah . . . I guess . . .'

'The name suits you.'

'Er . . . thanks,' I said and I turned away from him to look out
at sea.

There were a few other people from the centre at various

points along the beach, all of whom had brought their supper and were sitting, as Liam and I were, watching the sun go down over the horizon. Over supper, I had told him about my experience in the meditation session and I had done my best to make him laugh by doing all the voices in my head. Unlike Erin, he didn't appear to find it funny. He looked disappointed, like I'd let him down.

'You mustn't give up,' he said.

'But I am rubbish at it. I just couldn't concentrate.'

'It was the same for me my first time.'

I was surprised. 'Really?'

'Yeah. It's the same for everyone. Because, most of our lives, our focus is turned outside – nobody pays much attention to what's going on inside. It's only when you attempt to find stillness by going within that you become aware of all the frantic stuff in there. Like Sensei said, you have to go beyond it.'

'I *tried* to. I managed to focus for about four breaths and then I was off thinking about something. Nah. I just don't think that it's going to be my thing.'

Liam put his hand on my arm and looked at me with intensity. 'Your *first* time, India Jane. I wouldn't have taken you for a quitter.'

'I . . . I'm not a quitter . . .' I began.

'Sounds like you are to me. I mean, you wouldn't expect to master anything else in one session would you?'

He sounded like Dad. He would always go on about how, if

you were going to be good at anything, you had to practise — the way he did with his music. 'I guess not.'

'So. Give it another go.'

But it's boring, I thought, but I didn't say that to him. Instead I shrugged. 'Yeah. Maybe.'

'Really, India Jane. Stick with it. You've been given the most precious gift. Don't throw it away because of the shadows in your mind. They're not real. Like the saying, *the greater the light, the greater the darkness around it.*'

'Um. Yeah,' I said, although I wasn't really sure what he was talking about.

'Contrast. The greater the light, the greater the darkness. You are resisting because something inside of you recognises truth, recognises the light. It is the dark side in you that is resisting.'

'The dark side in me?' I asked. An image of Erin and I doing our zombie act for a laugh flashed through my mind.

'Yes,' said Liam. 'We all have a light side and a dark side. The dark side gives into temptation, leads you astray. It is like the weaker, lesser part of you.'

If you say so, I thought as I popped another little Greek cake into my mouth.

'It's like this,' Liam continued, 'the word meditation simply means concentration. Some people use a mantra like the word *Om* as a point of focus. Others use a candle or a flower. There are many other techniques that concentrate on the breath. I've tried loads of different types and this is really the best I've found. Stay with it, India Jane. Don't quit. Don't give up on what may be the best thing that's ever happened to you.'

I was beginning to feel confused and uncomfortable. I hated it if Dad ever accused me of giving up too easily on anything, but then he was a fine one to talk. He might have staying power when it came to his art or his music but, in other areas of his life, he was the arch quitter – always moving his family around the world when he got restless some place. I felt a flash of anger. I didn't want to be like that. But was I being a quitter now? Taking the easy way out or what Liam called giving in to my dark side? I didn't like to think that I was, but maybe I *had* decided to ditch meditation too soon. In the days before the session, Sensei had spent hours talking about commitment. Maybe I should try it again? It had felt OK when I was talking to Erin about it. Like no big deal if I didn't follow it through, but then she hadn't sat through any of Sensei's talks and heard what he had to say. I decided to be totally honest with Liam.

'I . . . oh, I don't know, Liam. I guess I'm feeling homesick and that's thrown me a bit. I really wanted to speak to my family, but . . . well, they were all busy. I felt like a failure.'

Liam nodded like he understood. 'It can be hard when you go within for the first time because you encounter how you really are, you know? Like, when you're busy with external stuff it can be a distraction – it can take your mind off what's really bothering you, but go inside and it's all there waiting for you.'

'I guess. All the voices. I hadn't realised how mad I am, nor how much I was missing everyone,' I said. 'At least, I *sort* of did, but didn't want to think about it, but anyhow . . . they weren't there for me when I needed them.'

Liam nodded again. 'You can't rely on anything or anyone in this world. It's a harsh lesson. Meditating can help you feel more independent. More self-reliant. Like you don't need anyone.'

I wasn't sure if I totally liked the sound of that. I would always need Erin and my family, even if they were all preoccupied at the moment. 'I'll think about it,' I replied. 'As you said, it was my first session. Early days. Maybe I'll give it another shot.'

'Great,' said Liam and he visibly relaxed. 'I knew you wouldn't give up. I could tell that about you and . . . well . . .' He hesitated for a few moments and looked out at the ocean, before turning back to me and staring deeply into my eyes again. 'I hope you don't mind me getting personal but I thought there was something special about you the first time I saw you. Special about *us*. A connection. Did you feel it?'

Not really, I thought as a wave of panic rose in me. I quickly checked that there were still other people on the beach. I so didn't want a repeat of the Robin experience.

'Er . . . I feel like we understand each other,' I said.

Liam nodded, then laughed lightly. 'We do. Hey, India, you can relax. I'm not going to pounce on you.'

I felt embarrassed. He must have seen me check around and the look on my face, even though I'd tried to hide it. 'I . . .' I began to bluster.

153

Liam looked away, up at the sky. 'I feel like we connect on a higher level, you know?'

'Oh yeah.' *Higher level I can do,* I thought and gave him what I hoped was an enigmatic smile. *Just don't try and snog me.*

'I was even thinking, like, maybe we knew each other in a past life.'

A past life? I thought. *Wow, this guy is so intense although . . . nobody's ever said anything like that to me before. It's actually quite romantic in a way . . . although I still don't fancy him.*

'Yeah, cool,' I said, but it felt awkward and I wondered if Liam had been about to say more but changed his mind when he saw how freaked out I looked. We both stared out to sea. I didn't know what else to say, so I got up.

'OK, Sensei's always on about being in the here and now so in *this* life not a past life, I think you're right. I ought to give this meditation another go, in fact, I'm going to go up to my room this very moment to give it another try. No time like the present, hey?'

A flicker of disappointment crossed Liam's face but then he nodded. 'Of course. Good idea. I'll walk up with you.'

Phew, I thought as we packed up and set off back up the slope. I felt slightly bad that I had used the meditation as an excuse to get away from him, but it felt uncomfortable sitting with him and he kept giving me long deep looks which I wasn't sure how I was supposed to respond to. If he wasn't going to pounce, why was he looking at me like that?

When we got up to the bungalows, Liam and I decided to go and get some mint tea before doing our meditation. Clare Taylor was at the dining area at the end of the long table with Joe and Rosie. She saw Liam and me and waved us over.

'And here's another of the new recruits,' she said, indicating for us to sit with them.

I braced myself ready for some banter from Joe and couldn't help thinking that he'd have laughed along with me when I told him about the 'voices in my head'.

'I'll go and get tea,' said Liam as I slid into the bench next to Clare.

'Had a good day, then?' asked Joe.

I nodded. 'Yeah. In the main.'

'Cool,' said Joe. 'I hear good things about this Sensei guy. A friend of my sister's did his meditation and it really helped her. She was, like, major weirded out by public transport, couldn't go on a plane or a tube without having a panic attack. She went and learned this method Sensei teaches and it helped her through. She's totally cool about travelling now.'

'*Really?*' I was surprised at Joe. Somehow I had thought he would mock it like Kate had but he seemed to be endorsing it. And I hadn't thought about using the meditation as a way to get through stressful times. *If I could get it to work, maybe it would be useful, like at exam times,* I thought. I could get major stressed at times like that and had been known to bite my fingernails down to almost nothing.

'Clare here was telling us that she had a wonderful session,' said Rosie.

'Oh I did,' beamed Clare. 'It's hard to describe but I felt so peaceful. It took a while, mind you. At first I was aware of all sorts of rubbish inside my head but I just kept bringing my focus back the way that Sensei said and, after a while, it was like my thoughts faded into the background, became distant and I felt myself growing still and then, oh, it was the most marvellous feeling.'

'How did you get on, India Jane?' asked Joe.

I glanced over to see where Liam was and he was still busy organising our teas. 'Oh yeah,' I said. 'It was good. Yeah, good.'

I didn't want to publicly admit what a failure I had been and that I had been thinking of giving up. Talking to Liam had made me rethink the plan. I didn't want anyone thinking I was a quitter and listening to what Joe and Clare had said made me think that maybe I *was* giving up too easily. Plus I had another reason to hold back. I was sure that I had already given Joe enough reasons to think that I was a total airhead. I didn't want to give him any more.

Chapter 14

New Era

The following morning, I woke in tears. I'd been having the most horrible dream and it took me a moment to come round properly and realise that it hadn't been real. I dreamed that I was walking down the street and Mum went past on a bicycle. I was so pleased to see her and waved, but she didn't see me. She rode straight past as if I wasn't there. And then I saw Dad and Dylan approaching on foot, both chatting away. I felt so relieved to see them and I waved to them too but they didn't see me either. It was as if I didn't exist. I was invisible to them. The feeling of loss when I awoke was awful.

As I lay there, I felt angry. Angry with Dad for sending me away. Angry with Mum for letting him. I felt helpless and I hated feeling the way I did. I'm not normally someone who feels sorry for herself. *Try the meditation,* said a voice in my head. *Go deeper than those roller-coaster emotions — that's what Sensei said. Maybe it will work at times like this. No harm in giving it a second try.*

I clambered out of bed being careful not to disturb Kate and made my way down to the beach. She'd been coming in late again and liked to sleep in during the morning. As it was early, I thought I might be alone down there, but I spied Sensei at one end of the beach and a few of the others, including Liam, dotted along at various distances away from each other. I sat down, assumed the lotus position, rested my hands on my knees, palms up, touched my thumb to my index finger the way I'd seen Sensei do, closed my eyes and once again began to meditate.

I opted for the first method that Sensei had taught and, as he'd directed, I focused on the cold air going into my nostrils and warm air going out.

In. Out.

Cold. Warm.

Actually not so cold as it's a warm day — so forget the cold air: warm air in and warmer air out. OK. In. Out.

Horrible dream. God it made me feel sad. I wonder what Mum and Dad are doing today. Don't think about it. They don't care about me. I'm not going to care about them. Focus.

In . . . out. Cold air. Warm air.

Joe looked so cute last night. He really does have such a nice mouth, with a full bottom lip. So much for Liam thinking I have a connection

with him. No way. I know where my connection is and it's with Joe.
He must feel it too. Erin said it's always a two-way thing.

You're not concentrating.

Oops.

OK. In. Out. In. Out.

Yes, the voices were still there, blabbing on about this and
that, but I was determined to go beyond them. I kept focusing
and refocusing, the way that Sensei had said.

After a while, I began to feel slightly more peaceful. Slightly.
And it did feel good when I opened my eyes some time later
and looked out at the ocean in front of me. I felt like my mind
had been spring-cleaned, the scenery all around looked sharp
and clear as if I was seeing it with fresh eyes.

After twenty minutes, I went up to breakfast with the others,
feeling lots more enthusiastic about it all, and I sat with Liam
and Rosie to have a bowl of fresh figs, honey and yogurt.

Liam beamed at me with approval when I said this session
had been better and when Sensei came over to join our table,
even though it was early days for me, I had a feeling of
belonging. For the first time since I'd got to Cloud Nine, I had
the sensation of having 'got it right'.

Over the next few days, I got into a new routine.

Up early. Meditate. Breakfast. Check for e-mails. Attend
Sensei's talk. And when Kate had gone out for the day, I'd get
my art book out and do some drawing in the bungalow, mainly

pencil sketches of some of the people up at the centre, but also some of the view from the veranda out at the front. I didn't show my drawings to anyone as I didn't want anyone judging them or me. It was my own private time and, curiously, I found that I felt more peaceful sketching than at any other time, even doing the meditation.

Mum and Dad had left messages to which I wrote a short reply.

Hi. Busy busy. Was homesick, but no longer. Have met my master. Am finding myself at last. Bye India Jane.

Part of me was still hurt that they'd hardly bothered to call in the early days of my trip and hadn't been there on the day I'd felt so homesick. OK. So maybe our schedules had been out of sync, but I had really wanted to hear their voices that day.

There was usually a daily e-mail from Dylan, letting me know some facts or figures about some obscure subject he'd read about, and I always replied to him. It was sweet that he bothered. I got the feeling that he was missing me a little in his own peculiar Dylan way.

And I wrote up everything that I could remember from Sensei's talks and sent it to Erin every day. It was as near as I could get to sharing the whole experience with her, but strangely she only replied once.

Dear Sister Margerita Bernadetta Consumatta O'Riley

I have read the holy blogs that you have sent and all I can say is:

oh *really*?

Call me when you have returned to planet Earth.

Erin

Hhm. I thought when I read her message. Clearly she wasn't happy with me. Maybe it was because up until then we had made so many discoveries together and this was something I'd done without her. Or maybe I just wasn't the India Jane she knew any more. I was changing and there were other parts of me coming to light. Maybe I was moving on from where we were when we were both in Ireland.

As I attended the talks and hung about up at Cloud Nine, instead of taking off with Kate and going into town, I got to know a few more of the guests, the reasons they were there and what they got out of coming.

Carey Freidman was one of my favourites. She was from LA and we got talking one afternoon while swimming down in the bay. I'd noticed her a few times at supper, partly because she was tall and stunning and partly because she always wore bright headscarves and I'd wondered why. She told me that she had worked as a model until she discovered that she had breast cancer last year. Although it looked as if she was going to make a full recovery, she said that it had made her rethink her whole life. 'The worst part was losing my hair,' she told me as we swam in the turquoise crystal water. 'I cried like a baby. And I know that we're all going to die sometime, but having an illness like this forces you to think about it. It makes it real. I can't believe I used to agonise over stupid stuff like what size I was, like it was the most important thing on earth. Now, I value such different things, like my health and my friends and family.'

Talking to her made me think about my priorities. What were they? A home, that was for sure. And Erin, who would hopefully still be my friend. But my family felt so distant. Like part of another life and that made me feel sad, especially when I met Anita Patel and heard what had happened to her. She was a slim, pretty pharmacist from North London and I heard her story when I went into town with Aunt Sarah to get provisions at the beginning of my last week. Anita drove us down in the centre's van and told us how she had lost her sister in the tsunami in Indonesia in 2004.

'Changed everything,' she said. 'At first I felt so guilty. You see, we'd rowed the night before she went. It was over some stupid little thing – she'd borrowed a dress and spilled red wine over it. I got so uptight about it. I never got to say sorry and that I loved her. What did a wine stain matter, for heaven's sake? Her death shook my whole world up, which is why I came here. I needed some time away from people who know me, who relate to the old me, because I don't feel like that person any more. I want . . . I need to find out who the new me is.'

I can understand that, I thought. *Even though I haven't lost a sister, I do feel like I am changing, leaving the old India behind and becoming a new me too.* Like Carey's story, Anita's experiences made me think. Dad and I hadn't exactly rowed, but I'd felt so mad at him for sending me away. How would I feel if anything happened to him before we had a chance to clear the air? The thought of him not being there, even if I was angry with him, was unimaginable.

Chantelle Harrison was an ex-footballer's wife who was totally glam – she even wore full make-up at breakfast. At first I felt intimidated by her and then I got to know her. She was a sweetie who liked to mother everyone and who didn't miss a thing. I met her when on kitchen duty and, after our first conversation, she took me under her wing and fussed over me like I was her long-lost daughter.

'Come here to find yourself, did you?' I asked as we chopped red onions for a salad one evening.

'No, love,' she said. 'I came here to *lose* my ex. I did bring his credit card, though, and the intention of running it up on a bit of me-time before I divorce the silly sod. And what about you? What are you doing here?'

'Not sure. My family sent me, so it wasn't exactly my idea. So . . . um . . .'

At that moment, Joe walked through the restaurant area to our left.

Chantelle nudged me. I tried to pretend that I hadn't noticed so she nudged me again.

'What?' I asked, but I knew I was blushing and that she could see that I was.

'You've got your eye on him, haven't you?' she asked.

'No.'

'Pull the other one, sweetheart. Chantelle's my name, Cupid's my game.'

'Oh God. Is it really obvious?'

'Not really,' she said. 'Only to me. I've got an in-built radar for romance. But don't worry, I won't let on.'

'Thanks,' I said. 'But, anyway, he's not interested.'

She tapped the side of her nose. 'I wouldn't be so sure,' she said. 'I've seen him watch you when you come into the restaurant.'

'Me? Really?'

She nodded. 'Really,' she said. She pointed over to one of the tables where a cute dark-haired guy called Pete was chatting to Carey. 'Like those two. They've been eyeing each other up for days too. Oh yes, Cupid's definitely flying about with his arrows around here.'

'Cool,' I said and went back to my chopping.

There were others I got to know as well. All with a story that came out as the days unfolded, meals got eaten and ouzo (the local drink) was drunk. (Not by me though. It tastes like paint stripper!) And the two sisters that Kate had said were lesbian librarians. They weren't at all. They were friends, Julie and Macey. Their kids had grown up and gone off to university, and both had felt an enormous hole in their lives so they booked to come here and learn to look forward instead of back.

Story after story of loss, upset or just a desire to find 'something more' came out. As I got to know more of the guests, I felt bad that I'd dismissed them in the beginning as a bunch of middle-aged losers and, as Kate had done, I had called them the 'inmates'. They were simply people, some older, some younger, but all were trying to cope with life and everything that it had thrown at them.

'Doesn't anyone here have a happy story?' I asked Aunt Sarah when I got her alone one lunchtime.

She smiled at me. 'You,' she said, then looked out of the window. 'Of course, lots of people do, India. But the centre does tend to attract a lot of people who are at a turning point in their lives and want to rethink the direction they're going in.'

I wondered if that was how it felt for her too. She'd separated from Uncle Richard, Kate's dad, years ago and, from all I had heard from my mum about him, he had been the love of her life and she had never got over him. She had certainly never found anyone to replace him.

Spending more time with Aunt Sarah felt good and I began to admire the fact that she'd set the place up. At first, I had thought it was just another business venture. Her canny ability to have her finger on the pulse and her eye on the main chance, but, as I watched her and her friend Lottie take time with all the guests and recommend various workshops or classes, I saw that both of them were genuinely trying to offer a service. A place for people to come and rethink where they were and what they wanted.

By the end of my third week on the island, I felt as at home at the centre as I had ever felt anywhere. Many of my fellow guests had turned from strangers into friends and become like a large substitute family. They certainly seemed more interested in how I was and *who* I was than my real family, whose communication felt more and more perfunctory and hurried.

'So what's your story?' asked Lottie one evening when a few of us were sitting down on the bay, enjoying the last warmth of the day.

'Oh, nothing compared to the others,' I said as I indicated Anita, Peter and Carey, who were paddling in the sea.

Liam moved closer and put his arm around me, which made me feel uncomfortable. He gave me a squeeze and then, as if picking up on my thoughts, removed his arm. 'So?' he asked.

'Nothing more to tell,' I said. I had already told him about my family and Erin and all the places that we had lived.

'So, where are you now, Cinnamon Girl?' he asked as Lottie got up, indicated her watch, waved bye and began to make her way back up the slope. 'What's happening now?'

I gazed out to sea for a while. 'Not sure. I feel . . . I feel like I'm in-between places, you know? I guess all of us here at Cloud Nine are. We're on holiday and that's always an in-between, like time off from your real life, but it's more than that.

I'm not sure about who I really am or what I want to go back to. Like I tried hanging with my cousin and doing the party girl thing and that's not my scene, but I'm not totally sure I fit with meditation people either. It's like . . . I feel in my head like I've left one part of me behind, but I'm not sure what's next. I don't know where I belong any more. God, I sound confused, don't I?'

Liam smiled and nodded. 'I know exactly what's happening with you. It's a process. One of the most magical processes on the journey of life.'

'Magical process? Doesn't feel like it.'

'It will. You're going through a metamorphosis. Like what a caterpillar goes through. I mean, can you imagine? There you are one day, crawling along the ground with lots of legs; you know your way around; life is pretty cool; you're green and then suddenly it all starts to disappear. You find yourself receding, caught in a cocoon, dissolving.'

I laughed. 'Yeah. That must be way scary, but last time I looked I only had two legs and I'm not green!'

Liam didn't laugh. 'I know that, India. I'm just trying to make you understand something,' he said. 'Imagine you were in a cocoon and you have to stay there for ages. Can you imagine what must go on in the caterpillar's head? Like, woah, help, trapped, don't like it. But it's part of a process, a process that moves him on and, when he emerges from the cocoon, he's not a boring old caterpillar any more – he's a butterfly with beautiful wings, and he can fly.'

'Yeah,' I said. 'I guess that is like magic, really.'

'That's what's happening to you, India. I think all these things around in creation are clues to tell us what can happen to us, to say, hey, don't be afraid when you feel like you've got the wrong body on; don't be afraid if you feel hemmed in; it's part of a process. The in-between. I think that's what's happening to you. You're changing from a caterpillar into a beautiful butterfly.'

It was such a shame that I didn't fancy Liam. He said such wonderful things and was kind and attentive – the perfect boy in so many ways, but the chemistry just wasn't there . . . He smelled strange to me – not bad, like he didn't wash, but like boiled butter. Not a turn-on scent for me. He was looking at me again with his earnest look that made me want to do something silly, like go cross-eyed and pull a daft face to break the moment.

'And you know the way out of that cocoon?' asked Liam.

I shook my head.

'Meditate,' he said and looked up into the sky. 'And then you'll fly.'

I suddenly had an image of Erin doing her 'I'm going to throw up' routine and had to suppress an overwhelming urge to lie back on the sand and laugh hysterically. Liam was *so* intense. And then I saw Joe go past and look my way. He gave me the briefest of nods and I so wished that Liam wasn't sitting so close. *Joe must think we're an item.* I tried to casually move away a little. I didn't want to hurt Liam's feelings – I did value him as a friend. I faked a stretch, then rubbed my leg and hobbled up. 'My leg's gone dead,' I said as I glanced around to see where Joe had gone.

He was walking back up the slope. He didn't look back.

Chapter 15

The Path

By the beginning of the fourth week, I felt I was more focused and a new, more peaceful me was starting to emerge. At least, that's what I thought. Kate was the first to let me know what she thought about my new-found view on life.

'Do you want these mags?' I said as I put a pile that I'd finished with on the end of my bed one morning after breakfast.

'Why? Are they too worldly for you?' asked Kate, lolling back against her pillows.

'No. I've read them,' I said, although actually she was right. I had been particularly inspired by what Sensei had been saying in the morning talk about people's need for constant stimulation and how it stole away appreciation of the here and now. I had decided to get rid of everything that distracted me, starting by giving away my magazines and packing away my iPod, and I resolved to only read books that were uplifting and, as Sensei said, 'were food for the soul'.

Kate looked at me for a long moment. 'You've changed,' she said.

'How?'

'You've become boring.'

'*Boring*?' I was surprised. I'd been expecting her to comment on how serene I'd become, not boring!

'Yeah. As in killjoy. And weird.'

'Like how?' I asked. I felt hurt by her reaction and the way she'd been treating me ever since I had joined the meditation group. She seemed to take every opportunity to put me or Sensei or one of his followers down.

'"Sensei said this, Sensei said that. Liam said this, Liam said that." Like you haven't got a brain of your own any more – or have you given it away along with your soul?'

'Of course I haven't. I've just found something that works for me. I'm getting a lot out of it.'

'Could have fooled me. You don't seem any happier. I don't think it's done you any good at all.'

'You can't judge until you've tried it for yourself . . .' I began.

'I bet that's another of Sensei's little sayings, yeah?'

I shook my head. Actually it was one of Liam's. He said that people were always so quick to have an opinion about people like Sensei and what he did, and they were usually people who knew nothing about him or hadn't tried his meditation.

I tried to focus on my breath and not get into a row. Only this morning, Sensei had been saying how we are so quick to react and if we just took a few breaths to calm down then we could go beyond anger and annoyance.

'Hey, Robin's been asking after you,' said Kate. 'I think he'd like to see you to apologise for that night on the beach. You should come out with us again one day before we leave.'

'Tell him apology accepted. I don't need to see him.'

Kate looked annoyed. 'So what am I supposed to tell him? That you're too stuck up now to spend time with the likes of us?'

'I'm not stuck up. How could you say that? I'm just into different things now, Kate.'

'Don't I know it. I hardly see you these days.'

'I'd have thought you'd have been glad not to have me hanging on.'

Kate shook her head. 'No. Actually I liked having you around.'

'You could come and listen to Sensei and learn how to meditate.'

'Yeah, right,' said Kate. 'I'd rather cut off an arm.'

She got up and started stomping about the place. As she packed her shades and cigarettes into her bag, I decided to leave her to it. If she wouldn't even give Sensei a chance, there was nothing I could do. I wasn't going to get into arguing, I simply left the bungalow and went to check my e-mails.

There were five.

One from Erin saying:

Oi, nutjob. Where 4 art thou an all and all?

She still doesn't get how important this is to me, I thought as I went on to the next one which was from Dylan. He had copied and pasted a bunch of articles about the dangers of joining spiritual cults. I was tempted to e-mail back something mad, like: Too late! I have shaved my head and given away all my worldly possessions and am no longer India Jane. I am now Sister Umbongobongo ji. But I knew that Dylan was a worrier and had my best interests at heart, so I wrote him a quick message back saying I hadn't joined a cult and he wasn't to worry.

By the tone of Mum and Dad's message, they had the same concerns as Dylan, but I didn't feel so strongly about putting their minds at rest.

India, please reply. We called but you were down on the beach listening to this teacher you mentioned. Sarah says you've been attending his classes. I'd love to hear all about it. Keep your mobile on between three and four and I'll call then. Love Mum.

Been a while Cinnamon Girl. Give your old papa a ring.

Let them worry about me, I thought as I read their messages and decided not to reply. Not yet, anyway. Aunt Sarah had clearly been filling them in a little so they knew that I was at least still alive. I'd let them think that it was me that was busy busy. *Me* that had a life. *Let's see how you like it,* I thought, moving on to the next one which was from Lewis.

Checking in sis. Hear you've joined a nunnery. Call the old ones and let them know you haven't lost the plot. Love the groovster Lewis.

I could tell that he had been put up to it by Mum or Dad. Mum probably. She was back in England now with Dylan while Dad continued with the tour. I could just imagine Mum, Lewis and Dylan sitting round the table in Notting Hill talking about me. Mum had probably asked Lewis and Dylan to be subtle about finding out what they could, but both of them were as transparent as glass.

Liam came in just as I was replying to Lewis and I filled him in on the various reactions from my family and Kate.

'Ah, yes,' he said. 'To be expected. Many people are threatened by change in those they think they know. Don't let it worry you. It is only the dark in them resisting.'

I nodded. 'I thought that's what it was.'

'You have to be strong, India. Be true to what you know even if it means leaving behind people who once knew you. You are

174

growing. Evolving. Embarking on the path. Kate isn't coming with you. When that happens, it sometimes means cutting ties.'

Fine by me, I thought. Through the window I could see Kate coming up the slope and heading off towards the shuttle bus. She was with Joe and I guessed by the way that she was gesticulating as though frustrated about something, that they were talking about me. *Say what you like,* I thought. *I'm moving on to a place beyond desire and beyond attachments.* I felt more determined than ever to stay on the 'path'.

'When I got here,' I said, watching Kate get on the bus and Joe heading towards the dining area, 'all I could think about was going back to London. Now, I'm not even sure I want to go back at all. I'd like to stay in Greece. I've found my place. My new friends. My new family. I want to stay at the centre and keep learning.'

'Not possible,' said Liam. 'It closes in October for the winter.'

'Yeah. I know. Just daydreaming, I guess.' I already knew that the centre closed because I'd overheard Lottie and my aunt Sarah discussing who was going to stay on after school started for Kate and Joe in September. They'd decided that Aunt Sarah would go back to London, partly for Kate but also because the run-up to Christmas was one of the most important periods for her shops. She might pop back to Greece for a weekend, but Lottie would stay on to manage Cloud Nine for the last few weeks, while Joe was at home with his dad. They had also agreed that, although both were in the Sixth Form and supposedly young adults, Kate was more in need of supervision than Joe. I didn't pass that bit of information on to Kate, as I thought it might start a world war when she and her mum had only just reached a truce of sorts and appeared to be getting on a lot better.

'So where does Sensei go?' I asked Liam.

'He spends his whole life travelling to different countries, teaching. Like he's only here for a short time; he never stays in one place too long. In fact, I think he's stayed here longer than he usually stays anywhere.'

'So what are you going to do when he's gone?'

Liam shrugged. 'Go back to school. I leave to go back to the Midlands next week. I have A-levels next year. My parents have insisted that I do them and they're hoping that I will go on to uni, but I have my own plans. I'm going to go to India and live in an ashram.'

'What's an ashram?'

'It's like a monastery. A place where there are no distractions. It's where you can really dedicate yourself to the spiritual path.'

'Wow. Sounds like you'd have to live like a monk there.'

'That's the idea. Maybe you should think about it too. It would be like full circle for you. You were born in India. Your name is India. It may well be your destiny that you go back to India. Maybe that's why you had to come to this place, to learn that.'

I felt a sense of rising panic. *Woah,* I thought. *Dunno if I'm ready for that — or is this a classic case of the darkness within me resisting the true path?*

176

'You could come with me,' Liam continued. 'You'll be sixteen by then. No one could stop you.'

'I guess not,' I said. 'But it seems like a big decision. Huge.'

Liam shrugged. 'Yeah, but from what you've told me, it sounds like all your life your dad has dictated where you go and where you live and where he wants to send you in the summer holidays for his convenience. You've always followed his journey and he's given little thought to yours and if it even remotely lies in the same direction as his. At last, you could choose your own path or at least spend some time in the ashram thinking about what it is that you really want. Come and check it out, at least.'

Maybe, I thought, though I wasn't sure that my path was that of a monk-type person. I had envisaged being more of a groovy bohemian arty-type person who shared a flat with Erin and gave fab dinner parties for interesting and creative people. Living with a bunch of people who dressed in white and got up at dawn to meditate hadn't exactly been part of my plan. But then, I hadn't known about Sensei or Liam or ashrams until recently. Was fate trying to steer my course in another direction? I wasn't sure.

'I'll think about it,' I said. 'Everything seems to be changing so fast. Like, suddenly there are regular messages from my family. Now that I don't care so much, it's like Mum and Dad have suddenly remembered that they have a daughter.'

'Yeah and what do they know? People who think they know you, don't. Especially family and friends. They expect you to act

177

and be a certain way and then, if you move on or grow, they don't like it, they put you down. It's fear. Fear of the unknown. Ours is the spiritual path. The road less travelled. A high and lonely destiny.'

'Yeah,' I agreed. It was certainly lonely – I seemed to be alienating everyone. Kate. Erin. Mum. But Liam made what we were doing sound so noble and even romantic.

'They're probably all getting in touch with you now because you've let go,' Liam continued. 'It's always the way. What you resist, persists. When you let go, what you've been repelling suddenly gets drawn to you. It's like a law of physics.'

'Yeah,' I said and got up to let Liam have the computer. 'Physics.'

As Liam slid into the chair at the desk, I decided to go to the art room and see if I could find some pastels to colour some of the drawings I'd done. Plus, I needed some time alone to think about what Liam had just said. Ashrams. Physics. It was all a lot to take in and feeling so uncertain about my future was very unsettling.

I was on my knees rummaging through the supply cupboard when Joe came in behind me.

'Hey,' he said. 'India Jane in the art room! Have you been working?'

'Oh! Yes. No. Not really. Nothing to see yet,' I blustered as I knelt up.

He sat down at a desk nearby. 'So how's it going?'

178

'Good. Yeah. It's funny, now that it's almost time to go home, I like it here. I've met some great people.'

Joe nodded. 'Um, yeah. You mean like Liam? You spend a lot of time with him.'

'I guess.'

'You seem pretty close.'

'We are, but . . . he's not my boyfriend or anything. Not like Kate with Tom.'

'Yeah. I saw them in town. They looked well loved up.'

'I think she likes him a lot. But it's different with Liam and me. I just like talking to him. He has an interesting take on the world.'

'Yeah, but . . . well, you don't have to listen or believe everything he has to say, you know.'

'What do you mean?'

'I've seen him in action. I think he fancies himself as another Sensei, like Mr New Age wise guy, but he's not even in Sensei's league. I reckon it's all to pull girls.'

'No way! That's so cynical.'

'Well, he can be very persuasive.'

I suddenly got the feeling that Joe had been talking to Kate and that she had put him up to this. I felt a flash of annoyance. *Did people think I was a total fool? First Mum and the boys trying to warn me off, then Kate, and now Joe as well.*

'I *can* handle myself,' I said.

'Yeah. Course you can. Just you seem to spend an awful lot

of time with him.'

'He's a *mate.*'

Joe looked at me quizzically. 'A mate? OK. Fine. Later, then.'

'Later,' I said. We both got up at the same time and almost knocked our heads. I didn't laugh it off like I would normally have done, though. I wanted him to know I was annoyed with him and everyone else for butting into my business like I didn't know what I was doing.

This way to paradise, I thought as I walked down the slope to my bungalow and remembered Sensei's words. *It's not as easy as it sounds.*

Chapter 16

Cross Examination

'Have you phoned your mum, India?' asked Aunt Sarah. 'She's been calling every day, but says your mobile has been off.'

There were four more days to go before returning to London and I'd popped into her office just after breakfast to see if she wanted anything doing. I found her busy as usual behind her desk.

'I e-mailed,' I said. I didn't say when. It was actually days ago and I hadn't even been in to check if she or dad had replied.

Aunt Sarah looked at me with concern in her eyes. 'Are you all right, India?' she asked. 'You look a tad pale.'

I nodded. 'Yes. Absolutely great. I've never been better.' Actually, I was feeling tired but I didn't tell her that. All the early mornings up at dawn to meditate, plus the broken nights' sleep when Kate came back in late, were taking their toll, but I was determined to make a go of the new routine and it didn't seem to bother any of the others. I wanted to overcome my weakness.

Aunt Sarah looked awkward for a moment. 'Do you want to . . . do you want to talk about anything?'

'Like what?' I asked.

'Anything's that's bothering you. I am here for you,' she said, then laughed lightly, 'even if I don't always appear to be.'

'Nothing's bothering me. Not any more. Honest.'

'So something *was* bothering you?'

'Yes . . . No.'

'Can I say something personal, India?'

'Yes. Course.'

'OK. I might have got totally the wrong end of the stick but . . . well . . . you seem to be kind of *earnest* about things lately. Not your usual self.'

'Earnest? Maybe. I have found something that means a lot to me.'

'Oh yes. The meditation group.'

'Yes. I've even been thinking about going to India and checking out about living in an ashram.'

'An *ashram*? No, India. Not you. An ashram is for a particular type of person, for renunciates —'

'What's a renunciate?'

'Someone who practises self-denial – not someone like you, India. I've known you since you were a little girl – you love life too much to cut yourself off from it.'

'Maybe I've changed. People do.'

Aunt Sarah didn't look convinced. 'Have you talked to your mum or dad about this?'

I shook my head. 'Not yet. Anyway I'm only thinking about it and I'll be sixteen next —'

Aunt Sarah still looked shocked. 'An *ashram*?' she repeated. 'But why?'

'I feel like the people in the meditation group really accept me and I might want to look into that way of life a bit more.'

'They accept you? Did you feel like you *weren't* accepted?'

'Yeah. No.' Aunt Sarah's cross-examination was making me feel uncomfortable to the point that I couldn't articulate. 'Well, I was sent here against my will, wasn't I?'

'Ah, so that's it. You're still angry about that.'

'Angry! Me. No way.' *Blimey,* I thought. *Another person who doesn't get me. Kate thought I was boring and now Aunt Sarah thinks that I'm angry! Angry. Huh! I was, but now I'm indifferent. I have so left all that negative stuff behind and am going the other way, towards peace. At least, I think I am . . .* 'Who would I be angry with? This place is paradise. You've been great.'

Aunt Sarah looked concerned. 'Have I? I feel like I might have neglected you after what you just said, and I know Kate spends most of her time with Tom.'

Ah, so that's why she's reacting so strongly to the idea of an ashram, I thought. *She feels responsible for me and doesn't want Mum blaming her if I run away.* 'Not at all,' I said. 'I've made loads of new friends. As I said, I feel at home here now. Really. I'm not angry with you at all.'

'I didn't mean that you are angry with anyone here,' said Aunt Sarah. 'Oh, darn it. Now I've upset you. Look, forget I said anything, OK? Just me sticking my nose into something that's not my business.'

After we parted, I felt unsettled by our conversation so I went to find Liam, who was now my total confidant. He was sitting on the veranda outside his bungalow, sipping a mint tea, and he invited me to join him.

'My whole life has turned upside down in the time I've spent here,' I said, taking the chair beside him. 'I had so many plans for my return to London. Good bits – like do the shops, explore the area. Not so good bits – like new school, the trauma of making new friends, being the new girl. But now I feel I've changed so much and I'm not sure how anything is going to be any more, not even going home.'

Liam nodded and poured me a tea. 'You don't have to worry about not knowing people – there are loads of Sensei's followers in London in your area. They'll look after you. We're your new family now.'

I reached over and squeezed Liam's hand. 'Thanks. I don't know what I would have done without you these last few weeks.'

Liam smiled. 'My pleasure. Look, I've got to go. Things to do, but you can stay here if you like. No hurry.'

'Thanks,' I said. After he'd gone, as I sipped on the mint tea, I felt an overwhelming sadness come over me. Although part of me felt good doing the meditation, another part felt empty. Lonely. I so wanted to be like Sensei, like Liam, like the other followers who looked so serene and glowing – not as Aunt Sarah had described me, earnest and *angry*. Angry! I clearly still had a long way to go on the path.

I stayed on Liam's veranda a while, did a little meditation and then went and did my chores up at the centre. After that I took some lunch and spent the rest of the day on the beach. I swam a little. Dozed a while. Walked along the beach and back. Then sat on my mat and looked out at the sea and sky. The earlier feeling of melancholy hadn't gone away. I tried to cheer myself up with thoughts about travelling to India next year, living in the ashram for a while. I didn't have to stay there for ever, did I? So it would be new. Unfamiliar. It would be both of those, but it would be *my* choice. *My* decision. I had to do it. Find out if there was anything there for me.

As the afternoon wore on, guests from the centre began to drift back up the slope to their rooms. I stayed where I was. I wasn't in the mood for company.

After the beach had emptied, I got out the stuffed pitta bread that I had left over from my lunch and was about to take a bite when, to my right, I was aware that someone was coming along the beach in my direction. *Probably one of the guests has forgotten a towel or something,* I thought, glancing over in their direction.

But something about the way the person walked, the posture looked familiar.

OhmiGOD!

'DAAAAAAAAAAAAAAAAAD!' It was my dad! I leaped to my feet.

'DAAAAAAAAAAAD!'

It really was him. My dad. Larger than life, like he always was. On the beach in Skiathos. Coming along the sand. *My* dad. He saw me and began to run and, when he got to me, he clasped me into a big bear hug and held me tight.

And then the tears started. Wave after wave. I didn't know where they were coming from but I couldn't stop them. Dad just held me and stroked my hair. It felt so good to have him there. To feel his familiar arms around me. To inhale his familiar Dad smell (a mix of cedarwood, lime and clean fleece). To feel how safe he made me feel.

After a while, the tears subsided and Dad let me go and held me at arms' length while he took a long look at me.

'So, how's my baby girl then, hey?'

'I . . . I'm good,' I said and then I laughed and looked down at the sand, because I'd just spent the last few minutes crying my head off as if I was anything but good.

Dad indicated that we should sit down, which we did. He put his arm around me and for a moment neither of us said anything. We both looked out to sea and then we talked. And talked. Although it was mainly me doing the talking. I told him about everything – how unacknowledged I'd felt, how angry about being sent away from London. How lonely I'd been and how I'd discovered Sensei and wanted to go and travel in India.

Dad looked thoughtful while he listened and he didn't interrupt or try to defend himself. 'So, why didn't you let me know all of this?' he asked after it had all come pouring out.

'I did. I swear I did, when we were in London. You didn't listen. You didn't seem interested any more. All I've wanted for ages is to stay in one place. Be a normal family with friends and a home, but no one seemed to care what I wanted. No one even asked me.'

'You say you want a home, but then you say you want to travel to India?'

'Only because . . . I . . . I need to belong some place and I thought maybe . . . I didn't belong with my family any more, that they didn't care about me. I . . . I thought that maybe . . . you didn't like me any more.'

Dad looked completely taken aback. For once my noisy opinionated dad was quiet. He looked so sad and then he took one of my hands in his. 'You must do what you have to and find your own path, but you must also know that you are more precious to me than my own life. My one and only Cinnamon Girl. I thought you knew that.'

Tears rose swiftly to the surface once more as I shook my head and he hugged me into his shoulder again. 'It didn't feel that way when you sent me here. I really thought you didn't care.'

'Oh, I care,' he said, 'and much of what you say is true. I was thinking of myself. I was. My job. How I would support my family. But I was thinking of you too. I thought, my girl's growing up. She's a teenager. Almost a woman. I need to butt out a bit. Let her go and not crowd her so much. I need to give her space to breathe and find herself.'

I sat back and looked at him. '*Space?*'

Dad nodded. 'I think I read the wrong teen manual. I got it all wrong. Maybe too much space, hey?'

The idea of my dad trying to do the right thing had never occurred to me and, as it did, the anger I'd felt towards him began to melt away. He was only human, trying to find his way like the rest of us. He wasn't perfect. He got it wrong sometimes, but he cared. He did. And that's what mattered.

Dad leaned over and pulled me in closer, so that my head was resting on his shoulder again. 'My only girl. I should have known better. India, I'm sorry. In future, we must always talk. Not leave it too late. Always talk.'

Before us, the dusk was beginning its nightly display with a blaze of colour lighting up the horizon.

'Another sunset,' said Dad.

'Our favourite time of day,' I said.

We sat and watched as we had before, so many times, in so many countries.

'I've missed you,' said Dad as the sun finally disappeared below the horizon.

'I've missed you too,' I said. 'And I've only just realised how much.'

Chapter 17

Homeward Bound

'Flight B413 will be leaving shortly from Gate 3,' came the message over the tannoy.

'Here we go again,' said Kate, slinging her bag over her shoulder, and together we made our way towards our gate.

I couldn't wait.

Dad had stayed on in Greece for two days. Spending time with him made me realise that the last week, since Mum had gone back to London, hadn't been a barrel of laughs for him either. Dad loves to travel, but with his family, and he'd been away from most of us and thrust into a new situation too. I wasn't the only one. Once we'd talked everything out and there was nothing more to say, I had a great time showing him the island. Aunt Sarah had let us have the car and we did the town, the beaches, the shops, the cafés, and at last I got to eat in the little restaurant that I'd spied on my first day on the island. The one with the stunning views over the bay where I'd imagined I'd be with Joe. So it wasn't with him. It didn't matter. Dad was great company and we had a fabulous time together. And then the day before yesterday, he had to go back on the tour, as the man standing in for him had to go on to another job.

I didn't mind when he said goodbye, because we were OK with each other again and because I knew that I was going to be homeward bound soon and he'd back with us all in October. I was really looking forward to being in London again and I hoped that Mum and the boys would be there at the airport to meet me. It would be so fab to see them all.

Robin and Tom had returned a few days earlier, so Kate was in semi-mourning, but Joe was on the same flight as us.

'No yogurts this time,' I said as he joined us on the way out to the plane.

'And how are the head lice?' he asked with a grin.

'Nicely cleared up, thank you. Not that there ever were any.'

'I knew that,' he said. 'It was fun winding you up, though.'

I gave him a playful punch.

Once on the plane, Kate took the aisle seat, put on her iPod, closed her eyes and was asleep by the time the plane burst through the clouds after take-off. As fate or luck would have it, I was in the middle and Joe at the window.

'Think I've got that feeling of déjà vu,' I said.

'Do you want to swap?' he asked, indicating his seat.

I shook my head and glanced at Kate. 'Wouldn't want to do anything to disturb the sleeping beauty. She needs to recover from her holiday.'

Joe laughed. 'And what about you? Do you need to recover from it?'

'Yes and no,' I replied as Joe took a look at the in-flight entertainment brochure to see what movies were on. 'I'm glad to be going back, though. Four weeks was enough. What about you?'

'What about me?'

It was the first time we'd spoken since the awkward scene in the art room earlier in the week and, this time, neither of us could get up and walk out. I decided to take advantage and to ask him everything that I'd wanted to know.

'Hhmm, Joe Donahue? Where can I start? OK. So have you always been such a loner?'

Joe laughed. 'Loner? Me? No. Why would you think that?'

'You kept to yourself a lot of the time up at Cloud Nine.'

Joe looked thoughtful. 'I guess.'

'Kate told me you're a party animal back in London. So what happened?'

'*Was* a party animal.'

'So, you're not any more?'

Joe shrugged and looked out of the window. 'Not sure.'

'Sorry. I . . . er . . . if you don't want to talk . . .'

Joe turned back. 'No. It's OK, India. No. Kate was right. I was the party animal. You name it, I did it. Drink. Drugs. Girls. Trouble was, there was a price to pay. My grades. My relationship with Mum and Dad, not to mention my relationship with some of the girls.'

'I'll bet,' I interrupted as I remembered what Kate had said about him being a heartbreaker.

'And to be honest, it was getting to a point where I wasn't enjoying myself any more, you know? You indulge in anything too much, it loses its appeal. Like at Christmas, too much chocolate and sweet stuff . . .'

'Noooooo. You can *never* have too much chocolate,' I said with a laugh. 'But I get what you mean. Like, yeah, you can get to a point where you feel, if you see another mince pie, you'll hurl.'

'Yeah. Too much of everything, and everyone over-indulges, thinking it will make them happy, but it doesn't. Your man Sensei said something one day that made a lot of sense to me. He said, if you seek happiness too intently through the pleasures of life, then you lose the meaning. But on the other hand, if you seek happiness through the meaning of life too intently, you lose the pleasure. You have to find a balance.'

'I like that,' I said. 'Like, moderation.'

'Yeah. He said some good things. I liked him. It was just some of his followers I wasn't so sure about.'

'Somehow, I get the feeling that you're talking about Liam.'

193

Joe smiled. 'Yeah. I've heard his routine – all that stuff about the darkness in you resisting when you don't want to go along with something he said. That's so manipulative.'

'The greater the light, the greater the darkness around it – that's what he told me.'

'And it's true on *one* level, but blimey, you could say that everything is the darkness in you, if you don't want to do something. Don't want to eat your greens? Ooh, it's the darkness in you. Don't want to go to school? It's the darkness. Don't want to snog me? Ooh, it's the darkness in you.'

I laughed. 'Yeah. Maybe.'

'You have to admit, he could be intense.'

'He was very persuasive.'

'And some,' said Joe. 'I guess we were just into different things. Opposites. But neither works.'

'What do you mean?'

'I did the pleasure thing; he did the opposite – the renunciation, denial thing.'

'Me too, for a while,' I said. 'Aunt Sarah said I seemed earnest. Kate said I'd become boring.'

Joe laughed. 'She's not the most diplomatic, your cousin. But a few times when I saw you in the last week, I thought you looked . . . well, a bit down, like you were trying to be happy but weren't, which is why I tried to warn you off getting pulled in too deep. I've seen Liam lay it on people too heavily before. But it's his trip, not necessarily theirs. That's all I wanted to say to you that day: don't let him talk you into anything you don't want to do for yourself. But Sensei, he was cool. He never tried to get anyone to do anything. He let people be, to find their own way.'

'I won't do anything I don't want.' I wouldn't either. I felt free of Liam and, in a way, a little sorry him. He seemed sad when we said goodbye before I set off for the airport. I think he knew that, despite our mutual promise to keep in touch, that I wouldn't – that, since Dad had been over, he didn't have the same hold over me – like I'd been awoken from the spell he'd cast on me. 'But what about you? Do you think you've found your way?'

'I'm getting there. Mum and Dad gave me an ultimatum. Shape up or ship out. I chose to shape up. I've one more year to go and then hopefully college.'

'Shape up or ship out. You never spoke about it. I thought . . . least . . . I thought . . . you —'

'To tell you the truth, India, at the beginning of the holidays, I didn't know if I was going to make it in Greece. Didn't know if I was going to stay or take off. Some days I was well ready to split. I needed to spend some time alone, to get my head together. I never really appreciated it before, but that place your aunt and my mum have got going really is a good place to go —'

'When you're at a turning point,' I finished for him. 'I met so many amazing people there who were at crossroads in their lives.'

'Yeah. Me too. That's what's good about it. People can go there to escape. To think things over and then go back to their lives. What I don't think is so good is when people run away and use the spiritual life as an escape from something. Those are the ones who Liam worms his way in with. Like he senses they're vulnerable or something.'

'Maybe. But they'll soon learn that they carry whatever unhappiness that is inside of them with them – you can't run away from it. Like with me, when I started meditating, that was when I realised what I'd been hiding from, I felt angry and lonely, but it was all inside of me – no getting away from it. You have to deal with it in the end.'

'Yeah. Happiness is a state of mind, right? I reckon you can be in heaven or hell on a beach in paradise, or heaven or hell in a busy street in rush hour, depending on the state of mind you are in. No point in running away to some remote ashram, like Liam is always trying to get everyone to do. I think it's because he doesn't want to go alone!'

I laughed. 'Yeah. Maybe. If he's going to go on the lonely path, he wants to be sure there's a whole load of people with him.'

Joe laughed too. 'All being lonely together.'

'Yeah. I'm going to keep doing the meditation, though – I just prefer to do it from my home in Notting Hill. I agree with you. I don't think you do have to be in some so called spiritual place for it to work – before I left, Sensei said that the challenge is to live in the real world and be happy. He said we have to be like a lotus. It has its roots in muddy water and yet flowers above the water.'

'I guess,' said Joe. 'Not getting pulled down into the muck. Nice image, though not one I'm going to be repeating to my mates any time soon. Can you imagine if I get off the plane spouting about being a lotus? They'll think I've lost the plot.'

'Yeah,' I said. 'My mate Erin thought I had, and I suppose I did get a little evangelical with her at one point. She really thought I'd lost it.'

'And had you?'

'No. I hadn't. Yeah, I went through some stuff. Like so many of us on the island, I was at a turning point too, but I think I know which way I'm going. Erin knows I've not joined the loonies, least not just yet. We talked before I set off for the airport, and she's going to come over and visit some time in the autumn, I hope.'

We spent the rest of the flight chatting and, the more we talked, the more I liked him. Like Liam, Joe sounded as if he had thought deeply about things but unlike Liam, I didn't feel that Joe was trying to get me to think like him. And he had a healthy sense of humour about it all. I hoped that he liked me too. I think he did as from time to time he'd nod his head, as if he was inwardly agreeing with what I was saying, and I think I did manage to get my thoughts across and be more myself and not the inarticulate idiot I'd been the first few times we'd met. By the time we got off the plane and collected our luggage, I felt like we had made a connection. A *real* connection. Like even though we'd only spent a little time together over in Greece, we'd shared something, a parallel journey.

'Be weird to be back in Notting Hill,' he said.

'Yeah. And it's all still relatively new for me,' I said as we wheeled our trolleys through the *Nothing to declare* exit into the arrival hall, where there were lines of people awaiting passengers. Kate, I noticed, was diplomatically drifting along in front of us. 'I was just starting to find my way round London before I was sent away.'

'In that case, I'll have to show you some of the good spots,' said Joe. 'I know where you are and I still want to see some of your paintings.'

'Yeah, cool. Whenever.' And then I couldn't resist. 'Hey . . . what birth sign are you?'

'Aquarius. You?'

'Gemini,' I said, and I couldn't help but grin because I know that they are both air signs and are really compatible.

'Gemini. That's the sign of the twins, yeah?' asked Joe.

'Or the schizophrenic. Depends on how you look at it.' Then I stepped to my side, looked at the spot I'd just been in and said in a deep voice, 'No, depends on how *you* look at it.' Then I stepped back where I'd just been and said in a high voice. 'No, depends on how you look at it.'

Joe laughed. 'You're mad,' he said. Suddenly he stopped

wheeling, put his hand on my arm and took a step towards me. As he looked into my eyes, I caught his scent, citrus clean, and I felt the butterfly flutter that I'd experienced the first time I'd seen him. He really did have beautiful eyes. Now that I was so close, I could see what an amazing colour they were – green with a circle of blue around the outside of the iris. I felt myself begin to blush. He smiled down at me and I closed my eyes and tilted my head up towards him. He was going to kiss me. I just knew it. It was then that I heard a familiar voice.

'Kate! India!'

I opened my eyes and turned in the direction of the voice. There was Ethan, about a hundred yards away, pushing his way through the crowds, waving like mad.

I looked back at Joe, who shrugged and smiled. His eyes held mine and he leaned towards me again. I closed my eyes for a second time and waited for his lips to touch mine and . . . there they were. On my *forehead*! I opened my eyes and tried to hide my look of disappointment. I needn't have worried. Joe was looking at someone over my shoulder. I turned to look. A handsome man in his late forties at the end of the line was waving at him.

Joe jerked his chin in his direction and took a step back from me. 'My dad,' he said.

I jerked my chin towards Ethan, who was giving Kate a hug. 'My step-brother.'

Joe took another step back and we both burst out laughing.

And then we looked into each other's eyes for one last time and just for a moment, it felt like we were the only people in the airport and I knew that he was feeling the same as me. Without breaking his gaze, he stepped forward and touched my hand. 'Later,' he said.

I thought I had never heard anything more romantic in my life.

'Later,' I replied. I managed to keep my face cool, but inside a part of me was doing cartwheels.

Joe began to steer his trolley towards his dad. 'I'll be in touch then, OK?'

'OK,' I said. I couldn't wait to tell Erin the latest. That I am Queen of Cool. Oh yes. That I had had a proper conversation with Joe without me talking rubbish. That head lice and spilled yogurt were a thing of the past. And that we had done the eye magnet thing three times!

And then Joe was gone and Ethan had taken his place and swept me up in the Ruspoli bear-hug welcome.

'You're very quiet, India,' said Ethan as we came off the M4 and headed towards Notting Hill. 'You OK?'

'Yeah. Fine,' I replied. Kate had nodded off again in the back of the car while Ethan and I had caught up on the latest. We'd swapped all the gossip and it was great to see him, it really was, but I couldn't help but feel disappointed that everyone hadn't come out to the airport to meet me, or Mum and Dylan at

200

least. I tried to shake the feeling off, but it was there at the back of my mind. I didn't say anything to Ethan though; I didn't want him to think that I didn't appreciate the fact that he'd come out to collect us.

The traffic was bad and London looked so grey and overcast after the light and sunshine of Skiathos. Everyone seemed to be in a rush, a mass of people earnestly going about their business. Watching them reminded me of something Sensei said in his last talk, which was that we have to learn to be human beings, instead of human doings who are always busy *doing* something and never stopping to just *be*. I made a mental note to make time to stop and be, by practising the meditation I'd been taught. To carry a little of what I'd learned in Greece into my London life.

After an hour, we finally drew up in front of the house and, a moment later, it started to rain.

Ethan told Kate and me to make a dash for the front door while he got our bags from the boot of the car. We did as we were told and, as soon as I stepped on to the porch, Mum flung open the door.

'Kate, *India*. At last! I missed you so much,' she said as she drew me inside and gave me a huge hug.

All my disappointment that it had only been Ethan at the airport evaporated away when I looked over her shoulder. There they all were, in a line, standing and grinning like idiots. My posse of relatives: Lewis, Dylan, Jessica, Lara and Eleanor. The adults seemed to be holding joss sticks or sparklers in their hands and, for some reason, the curtains in the hall were drawn which was strange because it was only five o'clock and still light outside.

Mum closed the door and Dylan went over to the light switch and turned it off, plunging the room into semi-darkness. He then scrabbled back towards the others.

'In place, Dylan?' asked Lewis.

'In place. And a one, a two, a three.'

Suddenly, four flames shot from four lighters and four hands lit the sparklers. Mum, Lewis, Jessica and Dylan frantically waved their sparklers in the air. At first I thought they'd all gone mad, then I realised that they were writing something – it looked like two or three letters each.

Seconds later, the words WELCOME HOME appeared in the dark.

The message hovered in the air in golden letters for a few moments, then faded away to nothing. I closed my eyes for a second and it was still written there, like a snapshot imprinted in my mind.

There was a knock at the door, Mum switched the light back on and Ethan came in with the bags. Then Kate and I were gathered up into a rugby scrum of family. Mum, Lewis, Jessica, Dylan and Ethan with Lara and Eleanor hugging our knees.

I was home.

Cathy Hopkins

Like this book?

Become a mate today!

Also available by Cathy Hopkins

The MATES, DATES series

1. Mates, Dates and Inflatable Bras
2. Mates, Dates and Cosmic Kisses
3. Mates, Dates and Portobello Princesses
4. Mates, Dates and Sleepover Secrets
5. Mates, Dates and Sole Survivors
6. Mates, Dates and Mad Mistakes
7. Mates, Dates and Pulling Power
8. Mates, Dates and Tempting Trouble
9. Mates, Dates and Great Escapes
10. Mates, Dates and Chocolate Cheats
11. Mates, Dates and Diamond Destiny
12. Mates, Dates and Sizzling Summers

Companion Books:
Mates, Dates Guide to Life
Mates, Dates and You
Mates, Dates Journal

The TRUTH, DARE, KISS OR PROMISE series

1. White Lies and Barefaced Truths
2. Pop Princess
3. Teen Queens and Has-Beens
4. Starstruck
5. Double Dare
6. Midsummer Meltdown
7. Love Lottery
8. All Mates Together

The CINNAMON GIRL series

1. This Way to Paradise
2. Starting Over

Find out more at www.piccadillypress.co.uk
Join Cathy's Club at www.cathyhopkins.com